MW01531216

ULTERIOR MOTIVES

amy hale

Ulterior Motives

Amy Hale

Copyright © 2015 Amy Hale

All rights reserved.

This book is a work of fiction. Names, characters, places, and incidents either are products of the author's imagination or are used fictitiously. Any resemblance to actual persons, living or dead, events, or locales is entirely coincidental.

Cover designed by Sarah Hansen, Okay Creations,

www.okaycreations.com

Edited by Paula Love

Edited and Interior Designed by Jovana Shirley, Unforeseen Editing,

www.unforeseenediting.com

ISBN-13: 978-1505891829

ISBN-10: 1505891825

For John, Matt, and Rachel.
Thank you for believing in me and supporting me in all I do.
I love you all more than words could ever say.

CONTENTS

PROLOGUE

Jacob Manchester sat at his desk and rubbed his throbbing temples. His thoughts had been spinning all night, and now, it seemed the room was destined to do the same. He knew it had to be the whiskey, and he was disgusted with himself for drinking to such excess once again. Jacob knew the news he'd gotten this evening wasn't excuse enough to drown himself in several tumblers of Jack Daniel's, but then he had never felt he needed an excuse. He was sure by now his liver was good and pickled.

Regardless, something important was nagging at the back of his mind, and he just couldn't seem to snag it back into coherent thought. The letter he'd found today wasn't exactly clear, but it was enough evidence to know that he should be very careful about who he trusted. He looked around his well-furnished office, hoping to find the object of his misery, but he wasn't completely sure what he had done with it. All his fuzzy brain could manage was that the offending object was missing. He leaned back in his expensive leather chair and closed his eyes.

The folder. What the hell did I do with the folder?

He was concentrating on that train of thought when a knock sounded at the door. Jacob leaned forward and placed his head in his hands, thinking he had imagined the irritating sound. Manchester Aviation was hustle and bustle until about six p.m., and then all would be quiet. He glanced at his watch and realized it was almost eleven thirty. No one else should be here at this hour. He heard the knock again.

"Hell. Who could that be?" he said to the framed photo of his late wife. Perplexed, he frowned down at his day planner as he heard the office door open and close.

Muttering to himself about a lack of privacy, he looked up from his desk. That nagging feeling became stronger. It almost screamed at him, yet all he could do was stare at the man standing before him.

Finally finding his voice, he grumbled, "What do you want? It'd better be good because I'm not in the mood to deal with you right now."

The man simply smiled but said nothing.

Jacob became irritated immediately. He managed to slur out, "Don't stand there and look at me like an idiot! What do you want? Can't you see I'm busy?"

The visitor sat down opposite Jacob and flipped open a manila file folder, still not having said a single word.

Jacob's eyes opened wide as he stared at the folder. "What are you doing with that?" he snapped as he reached for the papers.

The visitor quickly pulled them out of reach and shook his head. "Now, now, Jacob. We don't want anything to happen to all your hard work. It's best you let me handle these. You aren't exactly lucid right now."

The man rose from the chair and circled the room, the folder tucked beneath his arm. "You've been a busy man all these years. I'm impressed with how much information you managed to find. There was so little to go on after your wife was murdered, yet you've continued to pursue the truth."

Jacob felt the familiar sting of tears begin to form. "I loved her so much, and she was taken from us too soon. How could I just give up?"

He stood and walked to the window overlooking his private airstrip. From his third floor office, he could see most of the complex, and he always thought it was a beautiful view. His late wife, Mary, had landscaped around every building as if it were her own private garden. The roses were beginning to bloom, and the smell of rain had been prominent in the air all day. Of course, now, all he could see were the solar lights bathing the walkways in a soft glow, but he could envision it all in his mind. Soon, the entire complex would be a bright and cheery reminder of all of Mary's hard work. Despite the fact that he had hired someone to tend to the small gardens since she'd passed on, they were still Mary's roses, and they always would be.

Breaking from his thoughts, Jacob turned to face the man, who was now sitting in his chair with his feet resting on the desk.

"Why do you have my wife's file again?" he asked in a suspicious tone. That nagging feeling was as strong as ever.

"I just want to help. That's all, Jacob. You deserve to know the truth, and I intend to see you get it."

Jacob stared at the man for several moments, not sure why something seemed so wrong about this whole situation. *Damn. It has to be the whiskey.* He figured it served him right for drinking too much. He knew this would have probably made a lot more sense to him if he were sober.

"I appreciate the help, but tonight, I just need sleep. We can talk more tomorrow while I'm nursing a well-deserved hangover."

With a nod, the visitor rose from the desk chair and strode toward the door, file folder still in hand. Before he exited, he gave Jacob one last look and then walked away without another word.

An ominous feeling began to overtake Jacob as he once again sat behind his desk. Small bits of his earlier revelations were taking shape.

Someone he knew had killed Mary. Jacob would know more once he talked to the handwriting-analysis company. It was a long shot, but it was all he had. It seemed there was just one last piece of the puzzle to put into place, and he almost had it.

As he dozed off in his chair, Jacob's last thought was of his daughter, Elizabeth, and all she had suffered through since witnessing the evil that had taken her mother's life. As if he could see her standing before him, he said, "I'm sorry I've been such a horrible drunken slob of a father since your mother passed, Ellie. You will soon be free of all the torment. I promise." With that last whisper on his lips, Jacob passed out.

The next morning, Jacob Manchester's body was found among the remains of his 2010 Skyhawk. The details were sketchy, but it appeared that Jacob had taken the single-engine Cessna up after a night of drinking.

He had been known to take his favorite airplane for a short flight when trying to clear his head. Sadly, he had only made it a few miles from the complex before he crashed into the small wooded area leading to town.

Witnesses had placed Jacob at White's Bar earlier last evening, and a cabby had recalled dropping an inebriated Jacob off at the complex shortly before eleven p.m. The accident was believed to be pilot error.

Manchester Aviation shut down operations to mourn the loss of its beloved founder and president.

That same evening, across town, a man sat in a dark living room, illuminated only by the flames in the fireplace, and he smiled as he watched a manila folder full of papers burn to ashes.

1

Ellie Manchester awoke in a panic. She willed her eyes to adjust to the darkness as she scanned the room around her. Realizing she was alone in her bedroom, her heart began to settle into a normal rhythm as she threw her right arm across her face and groaned.

She'd had another nightmare—this time, involving both of her parents. These dreams usually just contained frightening glimpses of her mother being strangled—images that her therapist believed she had suppressed somewhere in her subconscious. Witnessing her mother's murder at age seven wasn't exactly fuel for dreams of lollipops and unicorns.

The nightmares had been less frequent in recent months—at least until her father had passed away. Losing him had seemed to trigger them once again but with a vengeance.

The last two weeks had been a blur of busy days, getting all her father's affairs in order, while the evenings had been an exhausting collection of sleepless nights.

Unlike the dreams of past evenings, this one had been jumbled, and she'd kept seeing someone's face—an angry face that she couldn't quite identify. Events had seemed out of order, and the final vision had been of her father in the cockpit of his Skyhawk with an empty bottle of whiskey in one hand. Suddenly, he'd screamed for her help as the nose of his plane dived toward the ground. She could still see him reaching for her as if she could somehow just pluck him out of the seat and change his fate.

"Oh, Daddy, if only I could..." she whispered into the darkness. A tear escaped and trailed down her cheek.

Sitting up and moving her legs to the side of the bed, she stretched for a moment and let her emotions try to settle. Switching on her bedside lamp, she spied the bottle of sleeping pills Dr. Andrews had given her. It had been a kind gesture, but she didn't want them. Even at times like this, when grief seemed to envelop her, she couldn't bring herself to take the medication. It made her feel more vulnerable and out of control.

Her need to feel in control was borderline obsessive. She knew that, but it didn't change anything. She couldn't always control events or her environment, but she did have control over herself, and that was all she needed.

Guilt tried to creep into her thoughts. She knew it wasn't her fault that her father had spent his last evening drinking himself into a stupor. Since her mother's passing, it had become a regular hobby of his. But she did wonder if she could have prevented the tragedy somehow.

The day of the accident had been an especially busy one for Ellie. She had used most of her day going over client contracts in her office. Working as her father's administrative assistant, she would often spend many evenings at her desk—kept company only by the radio, some less than stellar Chinese take-out, and a computer screen.

Jacob hadn't stayed around long that day, claiming he had some meetings in town, but during her brief lunch break, she had received a message from him. He'd said he had something to tell her, but it could wait until she got home that evening. She'd made a mental note to call him once the day was over, but by the time she had filed away the last contract, it had been very late, and Ellie had felt too exhausted to do much of anything. She'd sent him a text message explaining her exhaustion and promised to call him in the morning.

Little had she known, there would be no morning for Jacob Manchester.

Guilt once again washed over her.

I should have called him back before going to bed, she chided herself mentally. *No. There's no sense in hashing this all out in my head for the millionth time. It won't change the fact that he's gone. Nothing can bring him back.*

Ellie crawled back under the covers and rolled herself away from the light of the lamp. She needed to rest, but she couldn't bring herself to turn off the light. She couldn't deal with the darkness right now. It suddenly seemed as frightening to her as it once had when she was a little girl.

"Control your thoughts, Ellie," she muttered to herself.

She closed her eyes and tried not to envision the man lurking in the shadow of her dreams. But she knew he was there, just waiting on her to return to slumber.

The following morning, Ellie walked into Ted Bartley's office at Manchester Aviation and took a seat opposite his. Ted was a family friend, and he was practically a partner in the business. His focus was security and safety.

Leaning across the desk, Ted reached for Ellie's hands. "You look like hell. Have you been sleeping at all?"

"Not as much as I need to. The nightmares have returned, Ted. And something else…something new."

Ted slowly rubbed his thumb across the back of her hand in a comforting gesture. "New? What do you mean, new?"

"It's weird, Ted. The dream I had last night was a combination of my mother's murder and my father's accident. Somewhere, mixed in it all, was this face, an angry man, but I can't really see him. It's more like I sense him. It's creepy."

Releasing her hand, Ted stood and walked around the front of the desk. Seating himself on the edge, he looked down at Ellie. "Do you think it could be the meds the doctor gave you to help you rest? Sometimes, those can intensify dreams."

"No. I'm not taking them, Ted. And don't start lecturing me about it. I don't want them. I'll sleep eventually once the shock of everything has worn off." Ellie rubbed her temples and wearily looked up at the man who was more like an uncle than a friend. "But I didn't come here to talk about my dreams. I have a therapist for that." She put on her bravest smile and said, "What did you want to see me about?"

Ted stared down at Ellie for a moment before answering, "You don't fool me for a minute, Elizabeth Manchester. I don't mean to nag, but I'm worried about you. Your dad was my best friend, and you are like a daughter to me. With your parents gone, you and I are pretty much the only semblance of family we have left."

Ellie smiled at Ted, her affection for him showing in her eyes. "I know. I appreciate your concern more than you know. I just need time to deal with it all—preferably in my own way."

Ted smiled and held up his hands in surrender. "Okay, okay. I'll butt out for now. But if it looks like you aren't taking care of yourself, don't expect me to stay quiet. I owe your dad that much."

"You're a gem, Ted. I'm sorry if I come across as unappreciative. I'm truly not. Thank you for all you've done through this ordeal. I don't know how I would have handled all this on my own."

"You're more than welcome, Ellie. Anytime you need me, I'm here." Ted sat back down behind his desk and started sifting through papers. "The reason I asked you to meet me…" He sighed and ran a hand through his sandy-blond hair. "I don't know how to tell you this."

Ellie looked into Ted's troubled green eyes. "Tell me. Just spit it out."

Ted gave Ellie a sad smile. He always loved that about Ellie. She was great at acting tough when she felt it was needed, and she was stubborn as a mule. These traits were likely what had kept her sane through all the loss she had experienced. She'd simply refused to let it get to her.

"Ellie, I'm not convinced your father's death was an accident."

Ellie's eyes registered shock, but her face was mostly calm with the exception that she was slightly chewing on her bottom lip. "What? What do you mean, not an accident? They said he was stone drunk. It seemed pretty cut and dried to the investigators."

Ted ran his hand over his face in a gesture of frustration. "I know. It could be nothing. I just know that something about all this doesn't sit well with me."

Ellie was still for a moment, letting Ted's words sink in. *Someone might have killed my father?*

It sounded crazy to her, but Ted was the head of security for a reason. As an ex-cop, his instinct was usually dead-on. Still, she couldn't fathom the idea of her dad's death being intentional. She wondered if it was just paranoia on Ted's part.

"So, did you tell this to the police?" she inquired.

Ted grimaced. "I did, but the evidence is in favor of impaired flying, and my gut instincts aren't enough proof to launch an investigation. I can't even pull personal favors on this one. It seems I'm the only one who thinks this is fishy. But something isn't right, Ellie. I can feel it."

Ellie leaned back in the chair and closed her eyes. "What do you suggest we do?" She slowly shook her head as if trying to remove the very thought of the crash being deliberate. "I'm floored by this entire situation. Why would someone do this?"

Ted gave Ellie another grim look. "I haven't figured that out yet, but I'm working on it. In the meantime, I don't think you are safe."

Ellie let out a nervous giggle. "Not safe? Why wouldn't I be safe? I'm nobody!"

"Ellie, you are the new owner of Manchester Aviation. Your dad left you everything. You might not have taken over his duties yet, but everyone knows you are his successor. If his death had something to do with the business in any way, you could be a potential target. I'm not going to take that chance. So, to be safe, I'm hiring a bodyguard for you."

Ellie stood up and vigorously shook her head. "Oh no! You most certainly are not!"

Ted pressed his lips together in a frown and took a step toward her. "Yes, I am!" he said through gritted teeth. "This is not the time to be stubborn. Your life could be in danger. I'm not going to lose you, too!"

Ellie flinched at the pain she heard in Ted's voice. She knew this had been just as hard on him as it was on her. He'd mourned the loss of her mother almost as much as Jacob and herself. Her mother had been like a little sister to him. Now he'd lost Jacob, his best friend since childhood. It was almost too much for him to bear.

Stepping forward, she wrapped her arms around Ted and gave him a hug. "Please. I'll be fine. If I really feel I'm in any kind of danger at all, I promise you'll be the first to know. But no bodyguard. I wouldn't be able to stand the invasion of privacy or the constant reminder of this entire fiasco.

I need some part of my life to feel normal. It's the only way I'll get through this without falling apart. Ted, please don't take that away from me right now."

"You stubborn little brat," he said with an exasperated grin on his face. He lightly pushed her away from him. "Okay, I'll drop it for now, but please be careful."

"Yes, sir!" said Ellie, giving him a mock salute.

Ted hugged her again and then followed her to the door. "We'll talk again in a couple of days. In the meantime, try to get some rest."

"I will. Thanks again, Ted. And let me know if you learn anything new."

Ted nodded, and Ellie slipped out of the office.

Seating himself behind his desk once again, Ted opened the top right desk drawer and pulled out an address book. Flipping through it, he quickly found the name and number he needed. Reaching for his cell phone, he dialed the number and waited.

Ellie had just pulled into a parking spot at her favorite café when her phone rang. Seeing the name *Marcus Smith* on her caller ID, she rolled her eyes.

Marcus was her ex-fiancé, and he had been calling almost nonstop for the past week. Their relationship had ended badly about a year ago when she found him half naked in the arms of his barely legal female intern.

He had quickly become a successful lawyer for Edward and Associates, located in a neighboring town.

Ellie had figured he'd assumed she was too far away for any unexpected visits to his office after-hours. He had told her he needed to work late that evening, so she'd thought she would surprise him with his favorite fast food and her offer to help. She'd had no clue the briefs he wanted to work on were not in the file cabinet but in his pants. He had tried to explain it away, but she had seen enough to know she could never trust him again. Ellie had given him back his engagement ring right there with Miss Intern watching warily from her precarious position on his desk, and she'd told him never to call her again.

Over the last several months, Marcus had tried repeatedly to convince her that he had changed, but Ellie wasn't interested in giving him a second chance. She was cordial but cool, never letting him get anywhere near her emotions. She had let down her guard and paid the price. Ellie had promised herself that it would never happen again.

Since her mother's death, she had learned to rely on herself. She didn't need Marcus or anyone else making her feel helpless or needy. She was just fine and dandy on her own, and she liked it that way.

Sending the call to voice mail for what seemed like the hundredth time, she stepped out of her restored 1967 Ford Mustang and headed inside Mattie's Café. Finding her usual seat open, she sat down and grabbed a menu. Mattie, a matronly woman sixty-four years young with a plump figure and slightly graying hair, headed toward Ellie with a huge smile and open arms.

"Ellie, dear! I'm so glad to see you! How have you been, sweetheart? Are you eating enough? You aren't sleeping a wink, are you, child?"

Ellie was used to Mattie fussing over her like a mother hen, and she cherished it even if she would get scolded once in a while.

"Mattie, I'm fine. I promise. Nothing a bowl of your homemade chicken and dumplings won't fix." Ellie smiled up at Mattie, trying to put on her best I'm-a-perfect-angel face.

"Humph! Sure you are. Don't try that innocent look with me, girlie. I know when you're fibbing through your teeth. But I'll get you that bowl— with extra dumplings. You could use a little meat on your bones. And don't think this interrogation is over yet 'cause it ain't!" Mattie walked away.

Nessa, one of the waitresses and Ellie's best friend, brought Ellie a large sweetened iced tea. "Here ya go, Ellie, your favorite. Anything else I can get ya?"

Ellie took a sip of her tea and gave her a grin. "You know me well. Thanks."

Nessa started to ask Ellie about her weekend plans when the front door bell jangled. "Uh-oh," she said. "Don't look now, but Mr. Not So Wonderful just walked in, and he's already seen you."

Ellie looked up from her tea in time to see Marcus heading her way.

Great, she thought. *Just what I need right now.*

Marcus took the seat across from Ellie and gave his most charming dimpled smile to Nessa as he ordered a sweet tea.

Nessa bit back the impulse to stick her tongue out at him, and then she went to get his drink. She might have to serve him, but she didn't have to like it. Nessa didn't think Mattie would fire her if she gave in to the urge to dump the whole pitcher of tea on his head, considering what he had done to Ellie, but she decided it was best not to push her luck.

Ellie studied Marcus, taking in his chestnut hair, soft chocolate-brown eyes, and lean build. Then she gave him a stern look and demanded, "What do you want, Marcus?"

Frustrated and hurt, he reached for Ellie's hands, but she quickly pulled out of his grasp.

"Elizabeth, I just want to talk."

Marcus never called Ellie by her nickname. He always thought it was less dignified than her given name.

Ellie arched a disbelieving eyebrow at him but said nothing.

He frowned. "Really, I'm just worried about you. I know you don't want to get back together with me, and I'm done asking you. Seriously, I just wanted to make sure you were okay. Your dad's accident was quite a shock to everyone, and I know how much you loved him."

Ellie sat back in her seat and closed her eyes. *Why did Marcus have to be so sweet sometimes?*

She'd never trust him with her heart again, but sometimes, she did miss his friendship. So many times, he had been just what she needed when the sadness crept up on her, but that loneliness was a defect she couldn't let him exploit again.

"I appreciate your concern, Marcus, but I'm doing okay. I have Nessa and Ted to look after me. And Manchester Aviation is keeping me busy."

Marcus gave her a disapproving smile. "Sweetheart, are you sure you should be dealing with the company stuff so soon? Don't you think it'd be best if you took some time off? You know, to clear your head and everything."

Ellie instinctively flinched at his last sentence.

As a girl, classmates had called her Insane Ellie after they'd discovered she was seeing a shrink because of her mom's murder.

She was a tad sensitive with remarks about her mental state, and Marcus knew it.

Annoyance welled up inside her, and through clenched teeth, she bit out, "I don't need to clear my head. What I need is for everyone to leave me the hell alone, so I can get on with my life."

Just then, Nessa unceremoniously plopped Marcus's tea down in front of him. "Do you want anything else?" she asked, not really caring if he did.

Ellie knew Nessa wouldn't hang around the table any longer than necessary as long as Marcus was present. There was no love lost between these two, and Nessa was doing her best to hold it together.

Marcus gave Nessa an annoyed look and waved her away as if he were shooing a fly.

She gave Ellie a look that said, *Can I kill him now?* She waited for a signal from Ellie that all was fine.

"I think we're good here, Nessa. Would you please tell Mattie I'd like my order to go? I just remembered I have some stuff to sort through at Dad's house."

For a moment, Nessa's eyes softened at the thought of Ellie doing such a difficult task so soon after his passing. "Sure, sweets. I'll get that ready for you." After a final dagger-filled glare at Marcus, Nessa went back into the kitchen.

Marcus focused his attention on Ellie once more.

"Sweetheart…"

"Don't call me that!" Ellie snapped. "I'm not your sweetheart!"

Marcus pressed his lips together in a frown. "Sorry, Elizabeth. Old habit, I guess. But, honestly, are you up to all this right now? I just want to make sure you aren't spreading yourself too thin when you should be taking extra care of yourself."

"I'm doing just fine, Marcus. I don't need you to babysit me, so you can leave with the knowledge that you did your duty as my ex, and you are free from all future obligations in regard to my well-being. There—is that legalese enough for you to understand?"

"Elizabeth, please just hear me out," Marcus began.

Ellie stood, grabbed her purse, and walked toward the cash register with Marcus close on her heels. Mattie had just walked out of the kitchen with the to-go order and passed it across the counter. Ellie dropped a twenty beside the register and told her to split the change between Nessa and the cook. Ellie breezed through the door and out to her bright yellow Mustang. All the while, she pretended that Marcus wasn't behind her.

When she opened the door, he grabbed her arm.

"Let go of me, Marcus, or I swear, I will scream so loud they will hear me in Texas!"

Marcus stepped back and begged once again, "Please, Elizabeth. Please just let me come by tonight. I just want to talk. I can help you sort through your dad's stuff, if you'd like some company."

Tears welled in Ellie's eyes as she leaned in to put her food in the passenger's seat. "No. Just no. I can't do this right now. Leave me alone." She sat down behind the wheel and shut the door.

With a rev of the engine, she pulled out of Mattie's parking lot and left Marcus standing alone as he dejectedly watched her drive away.

2

Tanner Paxton walked into the waiting area of Manchester Aviation's security offices and took a seat near the window. He looked around at the lavish furnishings and expensive artwork and cataloged every detail in his mind. It was a little habit that had become second nature to him after several years in his line of work.

Pax, as his friends called him, had done his standard background check on this potential client, and he had found nothing unsavory about Ted Bartley. He was a confirmed bachelor, he had no criminal record, he always paid his bills on time, and from the looks of his office, he liked expensive things. All things considered, Pax expected this to be an ordinary job, but it never hurt to be cautious. He had been around long enough to know that what you saw wasn't always what you got.

Ms. Patricks, Ted's secretary, glanced up at Pax and gave him a sweet smile.

When he had arrived, she'd informed him that Ted was in a meeting but should be available shortly. Pax didn't mind waiting.

"Are you sure you wouldn't like some coffee or tea, Mr. Paxton? I'd be more than happy to get you something."

With that last sentence, Ms. Patricks batted her eyelashes a bit, and Pax realized she was trying to flirt.

Never one to let a woman feel completely rejected, Pax smiled at her with even white teeth and gave her a wink. "No, thank you, ma'am. Your charming company is plenty for me at the moment."

Ms. Patricks blushed, and Pax wondered if this nice but not exactly pretty young lady had ever had anyone compliment her. Judging by her reaction, he guessed it didn't happen often. He was trying to think of something to say when the office door opened and out walked a large man in a dark blue suit. His face was etched with lines that spoke of a rough life—or at the least, a rough past. Pax knew all about rough pasts, but thankfully, he'd turned things around before it could have gotten too far out of hand.

A distinguished-looking man with blond hair followed the burly man out the door and spoke in a clipped tone, "I'll call you soon, Harrison."

Harrison nodded his understanding and then quickly scanned the waiting area. He briefly took notice of Pax and then continued out the door.

"Ah, Mr. Paxton, I'm Ted Bartley." Ted extended his hand to Pax as he said, "So glad you could meet me on such short notice. Won't you please step into my office?"

Pax shook his hand, and Ted motioned for Pax to take a seat in front of his desk.

Ted then leaned his head out of the door and said, "Lisa, please hold my calls." Without waiting for her answer, he swiftly shut the door.

Taking a seat behind a large mahogany desk, Ted said, "Sorry you had to wait, Mr. Paxton. I'm interviewing for a few open positions here, and it's been a long morning. But I know your time is valuable, so I'll get right to the point. I'm worried about the safety of Elizabeth Manchester, and I'm looking to hire a bodyguard for her. I'm sure you've heard about her father's accident."

Pax nodded and said, "I know a bit of it. I've only been in the area for about a week, so I'm sure I've missed some details."

Ted leaned back in his chair and studied Pax for a brief moment. "My associates assure me you are the best in the business and that you're looking to relocate here."

Pax smiled. "True on both counts. Relocating is why I happened to be close by when you called. I was looking at some property north of town."

Ted looked pensive. "This is a rather unusual and sensitive situation, and I need to know I can count on you to be discreet and professional at all times."

Pax let the silence linger a few seconds, and then he sat forward and looked Ted in the eyes. "Mr. Bartley, I assure you I can be discreet and professional when the situation calls for it but only if I have all the facts. I don't do anything half-assed, and that especially goes for security details. I will guard Ms. Manchester with my very life, but it's important that you leave nothing out. I can't effectively fight an enemy I don't fully understand."

Ted smiled at Pax. "Please, call me Ted. And I think you and I will work together just fine. I'll answer any and all questions you have." Reaching into his desk drawer, Ted pulled out a large envelope and pushed it across to Pax. "You'll find most of the information you need in there, but I'm afraid this will be a bit tricky. You see, Ellie is very independent, and to be frank, she doesn't want to be protected."

Pax skeptically eyed Ted and then asked the question that had been burning in the back of his mind since the interview began, "Why do you believe Ms. Manchester is in danger?"

Ted looked at his hands for a moment, and Pax thought he saw a flash of emotion cross his face.

"I don't believe her father's crash was an accident," Ted answered.

"What gives you that impression?" said Pax.

Ted sighed and pulled a small key ring out of his right front pocket. He opened a locked drawer in his desk and pulled out a small stack of letters. "These." Ted tossed them on the desk in front of Pax.

Pax picked them up.

Ted began to explain, "I found these letters in the bottom drawer of Jacob's desk. They aren't signed, but they appear to all be written by the same person. It looks to be blackmail, but I don't think he was paying out. In the last couple of letters, the writer seems to be very angry."

Pax shuffled through the missives to find the specific letters Ted had mentioned. Reading through them, he noticed the writer not only threatened Jacob Manchester, but also insinuated that he or she wasn't past harming Elizabeth as well.

"Any idea what information the blackmailer is threatening to use against him?" asked Pax.

Ted stretched his arms out and then laced his fingers behind his head. "None whatsoever" he replied. "Jacob was a grieving drunk, but otherwise, he was a great guy, and I don't think he had a single skeleton in his closet."

Considering this statement for a moment, Pax replied, "Does Ms. Manchester know all this?"

"My concerns? Yes," said Ted. "I've discussed it with her, but she thinks I'm being paranoid. I wasn't comfortable with telling her about the letters though." He pointed to the letters in Pax's hand. "I don't know what those are all about, Mr. Paxton, but I refuse to sully Jacob's memory for Ellie. We can explain it all to her when we actually have some facts."

Ted stood up and walked to a file cabinet. Opening the top drawer, he pulled a large red folder out and waved it in front of Pax. "This file holds the paperwork that gives all of Jacob Manchester's assets to Ellie, including this company. There is a lot of money at stake here. Coupled with the letters, you can see why I'm concerned."

Pax scanned the information in the envelope Ted had given him earlier. "Money is always a possible motive," he said absently. Looking up at Ted, he asked, "So, just how I am supposed to protect Ms. Manchester if she doesn't want me around?"

Ted grimaced a bit and said, "I'm still working on that. What I do know is that she can't know you are here to protect her. It's hard to explain, but there will be hell to pay if she finds out. We'll have to be covert about it. Any ideas?"

Pax had a few, but he wasn't sure how easy they would be to implement. "Does she spend her days here?"

Ted nodded. "Most of the time. She has an office here in the main building."

Pax thought for another moment. "I have an idea, but I'll need to check a few things out first. I'll get back with you this evening once I've done some research."

Ted stood and walked to the door, holding it open for Pax. "Thank you, Mr. Paxton. This means the world to me. Ellie is like the daughter I never had. I don't know what I'd do if something were to happen to her."

Pax shook Ted's hand. "I'll keep her safe Mr. Bartley."

Then, he walked out the door, gave the secretary a final wink, and headed toward his Jeep. This job would be a challenge, but that was what made it so fun. He always thrived on a challenge.

Four hours later, Pax pulled into a parking spot at the Holiday Inn and turned off the engine. He sat for a moment and tried to process all the information he'd received on his new client. Ellie, as her friends called her, had been through a lot in her short twenty-seven years. He hadn't even met her, and he already admired her. According to Ted, she was independent, stubborn, and unwilling to take what life threw at her without a fight. Not many people would have dealt with so much tragedy in such a spirited way.

Getting out of his Jeep, he made his way into the hotel lobby and headed for the elevators. Lost in thought, he almost ran directly into Mrs. Hampshire, the petite elderly woman who managed the hotel. Standing a total of five foot nothing, she was a firecracker of a lady, and Pax had no doubt that she could hold her own with the employees and guests.

He looked sheepishly at Mrs. Hampshire. "I'm so sorry, Mrs. H. I wasn't watching where I was going."

She gave him a smile but pointed a finger in his face. "Mr. Paxton! You're gonna bruise up that handsome face of yours if you aren't careful!"

Pax had to bite back a laugh. She'd be surprised if she only knew how many times his handsome face had taken a good beating, and not because he'd run into a wall somewhere. He smiled back at the little lady and promised to be more careful.

"Oh, dear!" she said. "I almost forgot. A letter arrived for you about an hour ago. I have it behind the desk."

She walked around the check-in counter and pulled open a drawer. She handed the envelope to Pax, and he thanked her before walking away.

Once back in his room, Pax opened the envelope and studied the contents.

MR. PAXTON,

I THINK I MIGHT HAVE COME UP WITH A SOLUTION TO YOUR LIVING ARRANGEMENTS. AS IT SO HAPPENS, THERE HAVE BEEN A COUPLE OF RECENT VACANCIES AT ROSE HILL. SINCE THIS IS THE SAME APARTMENT COMPLEX WHERE ELIZABETH LIVES, IT SEEMS TO BE THE IDEAL PLACE FOR YOU TO SETTLE IN.

IF INTERESTED, I'VE ENCLOSED THE CARD OF DAVID BAKER, THE BUILDING SUPERINTENDENT. I'VE TOLD HIM YOU WERE THE SON OF AN OLD FRIEND AND NEEDED A PLACE TO LIVE FOR A FEW MONTHS. MAYBE YOUR LIVING SO CLOSE WILL HELP US KEEP HER SAFE.

TALK TO YOU SOON.

RESPECTFULLY,

TED BARTLEY

Pax looked at the card and smiled. *This could work.*

He sat on the bed and pulled out his cell phone. Dialing the number on the card, he mentally went over a list of things he would need to set up his new place. After making an appointment with Mr. Baker, Pax settled in for a good night's rest. It might be the last he would get for a while.

At promptly nine the next morning, Pax walked through the doors of the Rose Hill apartment complex. To his left, he spotted apartment 101 and the placard that read *David Baker—Superintendent*. He knocked on the door and then shoved his hands in the pockets of his sweatshirt.

After a moment, the door was opened by a tall middle-aged man, his dark hair sprinkled with gray at the temples. He wore a pair of dark slacks, a yellow shirt, and a somewhat eccentric-looking bow tie around his neck. Pax couldn't be sure without getting a little too close for comfort, but he was almost positive the bow tie had little stars all over it.

Noticing Pax's interest in his tie, the gentleman smiled and said, "Astronomy. I love astronomy. I was a science teacher for twenty-five years, but I decided to retire for something a little less challenging after my doctor informed me that I needed to choose between saving my ticker or teaching junior high students." He then stuck out his hand and said "Hi. I'm David Baker."

Pax smiled and took his hand in a firm shake. "Hello, Mr. Baker. Glad to meet you. I'm Tanner Paxton."

Mr. Baker smiled at him again. "Nice to meet you, Tanner." He then stepped out the door and shut it behind him. "Let's go look at those empty apartments. Maybe we can find one you'll like."

Pax stepped back, gestured forward, and replied, "After you."

Mr. Baker led Pax down the hallway to apartment 124. He unlocked the door, ushered Pax in, and began to rattle off the list of attributes and amenities. Pax listened attentively and nodded in all the appropriate places. He tried to pretend he was interested in the use of the gym and pool, but all he really cared about was the proximity to Elizabeth's apartment, which was upstairs.

After giving the basic tour and explaining the terms of the lease, Mr. Baker mentioned that he had two more apartments available, but one wouldn't be ready for an occupant for at least a couple of weeks due to the previous tenant letting his dogs run wild.

"Dang mutts," he said. "They made a mess in there. We have to hire someone to come in and replace the carpet."

Pax nodded his understanding and followed Mr. Baker up the stairs.

"We have an elevator," said Mr. Baker as he slowly made his way to the top, "but I prefer to take the stairs. Keeps me young." He winked at Pax and started for the end of the hall on the second floor.

Pax took note of the apartment numbers as he passed them. Elizabeth lived in number 231, and he needed to know where that was. As luck would have it, Mr. Baker led Pax to apartment 232 and unlocked the door.

Score! Pax was doing a slight victory dance in his head.

This would put him directly across the hall. He didn't care if this apartment was a hovel or a castle. He was taking it. It would fit his needs perfectly.

Pax spent the next couple of days furnishing and setting up his new home. He managed to catch a glimpse or two of Ellie while moving in, but it was always when he was already inside his apartment, so as far as he knew, she had never seen him.

He had given Ted a rundown of his basic plans and what stages they needed to progress in, depending on how credible or immediate the threat. Pax always had a backup plan as well, but he would play that one close to his chest, just in case.

While this wasn't a high-profile case, he never knew what someone was capable of. If someone wanted to get to Ellie bad enough, he or she might be willing to torture it out of her loved ones. He wasn't willing to risk that possibility, so the less friends and family knew, the better. In this case, it was only Ted, and he was an ex-cop, so that shouldn't be too much of an issue. But old habits die hard, and Pax's instincts wouldn't let him break protocol. He put a backup strategy together and started setting his plans in motion.

3

Ellie's father had been gone for three weeks, but to her it felt like forever. Somehow, it also seemed like it had just happened yesterday. She wasn't sure how she was going to make it through the rest of her life. She felt alone. Sure, she had Ted and Nessa as well as a few other wonderful people who had always been there for her, but it just wasn't the same as having blood relatives.

While Jacob hadn't exactly been father of the year, through it all, she had known he loved her. That love had kept her going many times, even when she couldn't physically depend on him. She'd lost count of the times, as a young girl, when she had sought her dad out, only to find him passed out in the den with an empty whiskey or gin bottle nearby. So, she'd sit somewhere near him, hold his hand or touch his arm, and just listen to him snore. It hadn't been much, but she had been with him, and she'd found it oddly comforting.

Ellie stood in her living room with the early morning light streaming through the windows and bathing everything in a golden glow. She stared down at the box sitting on her coffee table, full of personal items that had been removed from Jacob's office, but she couldn't bring herself to go through them. She just didn't have the heart or maybe the courage to deal with it right now.

Making her way to the kitchen, she washed out her morning coffee cup and put it away. Ellie spent a few moments just staring at the floor, trying to decide what to do with herself on such a glorious Saturday morning. Breezy seventy-five degree days were a treat for Oklahoma in June, so she wasn't about to spend it indoors, moping over her father's belongings. Finally deciding, she changed into her running clothes and headed out the door with a heavy sigh.

Ellie had just locked up and turned around in a bit of a hurry when she ran into something solid. To her horror, it wasn't something but someone, and he'd been holding a full cup of coffee. The cup was no longer full, but instead, it was all over the front of his shirt and jeans.

"Oh, no! I'm so sorry!"

He attempted to hold the wet shirt away from his chest.

"Please tell me you aren't burned!"

The stranger smiled at her, and her tummy did little flips. She found herself slightly stunned by her body's response to that one small action.

She'd noticed right away that he was a handsome man, but when he smiled, it felt as if all the oxygen had been depleted from the air. His neatly cut dark hair was in stark contrast to his piercing blue eyes. He had a small dimple when he smiled, and his chin was strong and slightly squared. A small scar on his cheek marred an otherwise perfect face. He absentmindedly scratched at his day-old stubble as he quickly looked her over. She felt she was under an inspection of some kind, and it made her suddenly nervous.

"No, the coffee was only warm, so no serious damage done." He smiled again with even white teeth and introduced himself, "Hi, I'm Tanner Paxton, but please call me Pax. I just moved in across the hall."

Ellie smiled back and took his offered handshake. "Nice to meet you. I'm Elizabeth Manchester. Welcome to Rose Hill."

Pax stepped back and then looked down at his soaked jeans and red T-shirt. "I guess I'd better go change," he said with a smirk.

Ellie had temporarily forgotten about her clumsy collision and began to apologize again, "I'm so, so sorry. I promise not to run you over every time I leave my apartment. I'm just a little distracted today. I should have been more careful."

Pax studied her for a brief moment before saying, "Really, it's no problem at all." He really wanted to say *Please run me over as often as you like.*

He'd seen a photo of Ellie in the job folder, but he hadn't been prepared to like her so much. Something had drawn him in from the moment she'd slammed into him. *Honestly, what red-blooded man wouldn't be attracted to someone like Elizabeth Manchester?* Her long reddish-brown curls fell midway down her back, and her eyes were almost a chocolate brown, framed by satiny long lashes. She had high cheekbones and full pink lips that he was certain he'd think about long after they parted ways today. She was a petite woman at five-four, and her yoga pants and tank top showcased her curves nicely.

Uncomfortable with the directions his thoughts were taking, he cleared his throat and tried to focus on his mission—befriend Elizabeth Manchester.

She smiled at him a little sheepishly and said, "Well, I'm still very sorry. I hope I didn't ruin your clothes."

Pax glanced down at himself once more. "I'm sure they'll be fine. I could use another cup of coffee though."

Ellie laughed. "Please let me buy you a cup. I owe you that much."

Looking at his watch, Pax replied, "Sounds like a deal. But it looks like you were on your way out, and I have some errands to run. How about a rain check?"

"Sure," said Ellie. "Just let me know when, and that coffee is all yours." She tossed a chirpy, "See you later!" over her shoulder as she made her way down the hall to the stairway.

Pax smiled to himself as he crossed the threshold of his own apartment and shut the door behind him. "If I have it my way, you'll be seeing a lot of me, Ellie," he said to himself. Then, he pulled his stained T-shirt over his head and walked toward his bedroom to quickly change.

Ellie was on her third lap around the track at the park before she realized she wasn't really paying attention to her heart rate. Her mind was elsewhere—specifically on a handsome guy she had accidentally doused in warm coffee. Her cheeks flamed with humiliation as she recalled the incident.

Why, of all days, did I have to be so out of it?

She felt like fate was determined to make her miserable. Hopefully, Pax wasn't too upset about the collision and really did want that cup of coffee she'd offered. While she wasn't interested in a relationship, it would be nice to be on friendly terms with her newest neighbor.

The elderly lady next door was pretty cranky and kept to herself, except when complaining about something, and Ellie rarely saw the other tenant across the hall. From what she understood, he was one of those really smart tech guys, and he traveled the world, setting up computer systems, so he was never home.

Giving up all pretense of caring about her run, she started walking the few blocks back to her apartment. Waiting for a light to change, she glanced down at her watch to check the time. When all was clear, she started to cross the street, but things quickly took a turn for the worse.

One moment, she was taking a step off the curb, and the next, she was flat on her back with a rather muscular arm wrapped around her waist in a protective fashion. She faintly registered the sound of squealing tires as she tried to catch her breath.

"What the hell?" she managed to wheeze out between gasps for air.

Attempting to sit up, she realized the arm belonged to Pax.

"Are you okay?" he asked as he began to look her over for injuries.

"I had the wind knocked out of me, but otherwise, I think I'm fine. What just happened?"

Pax's lips pressed together in a grim line. "You were almost hit by that truck."

"Truck?" Ellie said in confusion.

She didn't recall seeing a truck anywhere around that corner. She must have really been distracted to be so careless. *Stupid-ass hormones. I'm going to have to get a grip before I kill myself.*

Pax helped her to her feet, and she brushed off the back of her arms. Ellie stilled as Pax started brushing the dirt from the back of her shirt. He was only being helpful, but it felt too personal. It felt too good. His touch should not be causing shivers down her spine.

For crap's sake, I don't even know the man!

She closed her eyes and groaned at how pathetic she must seem. Pax misinterpreted her groan for pain and began to gingerly touch her arms, again looking for any sign of injury.

She held up her hands. "I'm fine—really. I just can't believe this happened. I promise, I'm not usually this accident-prone."

He smiled at her, but it didn't quite reach his eyes. "I'm sure you aren't. We all have bad days. Are you heading back home?"

Ellie nodded.

"Me too," he said. "I'll walk with you."

Side by side, they made the rest of the short walk to Rose Hill. Pax asked her a couple of questions about the community, and she gladly answered. She was grateful for any topic that would fill the silence and keep them from discussing her recent bout of clumsiness.

Once inside the building, she dug a key out of the small zipper pocket in her pants and made her way up the stairs. Pax was close behind, and she could almost feel his eyes on her.

Reaching her door, she turned around gave him a small smile. "Listen, I haven't thanked you yet for pulling me out of harm's way. If it weren't for you getting to me so quickly, I…"

She stopped. *How did Pax get to me so fast? Where had he been? It seemed as if he had come out of nowhere, just like the truck. However he'd done it, thank God he had been there.*

"Anyway, thank you. A hospital stay would've put a real damper on the rest of my weekend."

Pax chuckled. "Yeah, I'm sure it would have."

Ellie considered inviting him in for the promised coffee, but she decided that might not be the best idea right now. She was still rattled from her close call. She needed a shower, and her reaction to him was a tad worrisome. Maybe some distance was a better idea for the moment. She was mentally arguing the pros and cons when Pax solved the matter for her.

"Well, if you're really okay, Elizabeth, I've got an appointment to keep, and I need to get my stuff together."

Ellie smiled at him again. "I'm perfectly okay. And please call me Ellie." She made a show of scanning her disheveled appearance. "I think I'm gonna take a hot shower and catch up on some reading. Hopefully, I can't hurt myself that way."

Pax laughed again. "Have a great afternoon Ellie." Then, he disappeared behind his apartment door.

Ellie slipped into her apartment and headed straight for the shower. The hot water was going to feel good on her sore spots.

Across the hall, Pax was considering taking a shower as well but a cold one. The image of Ellie in the shower with water running down her naked body was causing him some discomfort. He didn't need this kind of attraction. He had sworn off any kind of relationship years ago when he realized he couldn't effectively do his job and keep a girlfriend happy at the same time. While he wasn't against short flings and a little fun, this was not the time—or the girl. He needed his wits about him to keep her safe. He'd been on the job for less than forty-eight hours, and already, someone had tried to run her down. He was sure that truck careening out of nowhere had not been an accident.

Mentally, he replayed the events of the morning. He had quickly changed out of his coffee-stained clothes and headed out to follow Ellie. He had been discreet and far enough behind that she'd never noticed him there. Pax had watched her run her laps while he had taken note of the surroundings. When she'd stopped mid-run on the third lap, he had been concerned that something was wrong, but when she'd turned around and headed back toward home, she'd just looked annoyed.

He'd again followed behind her as she approached the intersection. Pax had noticed the light change from green to yellow, and then he'd heard it— the sound of an engine revving. He had gotten closer in case she would need him. He had just been a few feet behind her when he saw the beat-up green Chevy truck heading right toward her. He had sprung into action, grabbing her around the waist and pulling her backward. They'd landed on the sidewalk. Or more accurately, he'd landed on the sidewalk, and she'd bounced off of him and then hit the concrete. At least his body had shielded the brunt of the blow for her, and she hadn't had any real injuries to speak of.

He had been so focused on getting her out of the way that he'd missed most of the Chevy's license plate.

He needed to talk to Ted as soon as possible. It was time to implement part two of his plan. Picking up the phone, he called Ted and set up a quick meeting. Then, he entered the bathroom for that cold shower.

Ted pulled up to Manchester Aviation and put his black BMW in park. The lot was empty, except for Pax, who was leaning against the door of his Jeep with his arms crossed. Ted got out and leaned against his own vehicle.

The look on Pax's face made him uneasy. Something had happened, something bad.

Pax stood up and took a few steps toward Ted. Pax handed him a slip of paper. Eyebrows raised, Ted looked down to see he was holding the description of a truck with partial plate numbers.

"Know anyone with a truck fitting that description?" Pax asked.

Ted slowly shook his head. "No. Why? What happened? Is Ellie okay?"

Pax could hear the worried tone in Ted's voice. He placed a hand on Ted's shoulder. "She's fine, but it was close. That truck almost mowed her down about a block from the apartments. I got to her just in time."

Ted's face fell. "Any chance it was an accident?" One look at Pax's grim expression told him all he needed to know. "No, I suppose not." Sighing, Ted continued on, "I was really hoping I was wrong about this, but now, I'm sure hiring you was the right thing to do even if Ellie refuses to see it herself."

Pax stuffed his hands in the pockets of his jeans. "Ted, are you sure we can't tell Ellie the truth about me? Maybe, after today, she'd understand."

Ted shook his head. "No, she's bullheaded, and it'll take something major to convince her that she's in danger. Hell, even then, she'd probably argue about it."

After a moment of silence, Pax turned and walked back to his Jeep. He placed both of his palms on the hood and stared into the windshield, momentarily lost in thought. "I think it's important to move forward with the next stage."

Ted nodded in agreement. "Yes, I agree. Your badge and security key will be waiting at the front desk. Welcome to Manchester Aviation, Mr. Paxton. You have no idea how happy I am to have you on board."

4

Monday morning, Ellie walked into the lobby of Manchester Aviation and approached the reception desk. She gave a sunny smile to the receptionist, Christin, a twenty-four-year-old with long blonde hair and a plump figure, thanks to impending motherhood.

"How was your weekend?" asked Ellie.

"I slept most of the weekend," said Christin. "This whole pregnancy thing is exhausting." Reaching down to her ever growing belly, she gave it an absentminded scratch.

"How far along are you?" Ellie asked as she dug in her purse for her key card.

"Six months, but it feels like I've been preggers forever," replied Christin.

"It can't be all that bad." Ellie chuckled.

"It's really not," Christin admitted. "I'm just tired of feeling like a cow, especially when we have a new hot guy on staff. Have you seen him yet? Whew!" she said, dramatically fanning herself.

Ellie didn't remember hearing about the newest employee, but she did remember Ted conducting interviews a few weeks back. "No, but I'm sure I'll meet him soon," she replied.

Christin waggled her eyebrows and said, "Hubba, hubba!"

Ellie laughed. "Don't let Jeff hear you say that. He might make you quit, and we need you here."

Christin rolled her eyes. "Yeah, like he could really make me do anything. Everyone knows I wear the pants in our family. I just let him think he's the boss."

The phone rang and interrupted their conversation. Christin picked up the receiver and winked at Ellie, who gave her a wave as she headed toward the elevators. She stood, waiting on the doors to open, when she heard a familiar voice behind her.

"Fancy meeting you here."

She turned to see Pax standing casually in a pair of tan Dockers and a white polo shirt with Manchester Aviation's initials embroidered above the left breast. She'd never considered those shirts appealing in any way, but Pax made it look sexy. It didn't hurt that his biceps, wide shoulders, and noticeably defined pectoral muscles bulged under the tight-fitting fabric.

"Hi. What are you doing here?" she squeaked out, wondering why her voice was suddenly abandoning her.

Pax pointed to the logo on his shirt. "I just started today. I was hired as part of the new security team Mr. Bartley is putting together." Feigning a confused look, he smacked his head with the palm of his hand. "I can't believe I didn't put two and two together the other day. Elizabeth Manchester. You must be my new boss."

Ellie shook her head. "No, Ted's really your boss. I have the name, and technically, I inherited the business, but Ted is the man with the plan. He was my dad's right-hand man for years. I just follow along."

At that moment, the elevator doors opened, and Ellie stepped in.

"Going up?" she asked. Part of her hoped he was staying on the first floor, but the more traitorous part of her wanted a few more minutes alone with him. Her heart raced at the thought of Pax joining her in the enclosed small space. She mentally kicked herself for the naughty images flashing in her mind. *This will never do*, she silently chided herself.

Pax stepped into the elevator with her. Lost in thoughts she shouldn't be having, she forgot to insert her security key and press the third-floor button. Pax reached across her, put his card in the key slot, and then pushed the number three. For a moment, his face was so close to hers that she could smell his cologne and feel his breath on her neck.

As he pulled back, he softly said, "Excuse me," in her ear.

She nodded silently and took one step to the left. She would have moved even more, but she was afraid it would be obvious if she did.

Pax hid a secretive smile. He'd heard that small hitch in her breathing when he moved close to her. He knew she wasn't as unaffected as she pretended, and even though it shouldn't have pleased him, his male pride was doing peacock struts in his head.

When the doors opened to their floor, Ellie hurriedly stepped out and headed toward her office. Realizing she'd forgotten her manners, she turned back to him.

"It was good to see you again. I hope you enjoy working here." Then, she disappeared into her office and shut the door behind her.

Pax couldn't help but wonder if she was running from him or from herself.

About an hour later, Ted walked into Ellie's office with an armload of paperwork. She glanced up from her computer as he handed her a new contract.

"Hold on, Ted. I need to talk to you."

Ted nodded, shut her office door, and took a seat on the edge of her desk. "What's up, buttercup?"

Ellie couldn't help but grin at his term of endearment. Ted had called her buttercup when she was a little girl, but he hadn't referred to her in that way in years.

"Did you hire two people for the job opening we were advertising for? I thought you were just looking for one person."

Ted looked confused for a moment, and then it hit him. She must be talking about Pax. He cleared his throat, hating to lie to her, but he knew it was necessary for her own safety. "No. I only hired one person for that job—James Lincoln. You met him last week."

Ellie nodded, remembering the tall blond young man who barely looked old enough to be out of high school.

Ted continued, "I did, however, hire another guy on my security staff. His name is Tanner Paxton."

Ellie nodded once again. "Yeah, I've met him."

Without waiting for her to elaborate, Ted continued to explain his actions, hoping she wouldn't see through his next lie. "Honestly, Pax is the kid of an old friend of mine. Security has become his specialty over the years, and I thought he could help me upgrade this place. I hired him as a consultant of sorts. Our guys could learn a lot from him, too."

Ellie thought that made sense although she personally didn't see a reason to do much upgrading to their current security systems. So far, they hadn't encountered any issues. From what she could tell, Ted had dropped this silly business about her being in danger. But if it made him feel better to upgrade security, she wasn't going to deny him that comfort. *My dad had put Ted in charge of all that for a reason, so who am I to argue with him?*

"I see. I was just surprised. Pax is also my new neighbor, so I didn't expect to see him here as well."

Ted thought he'd heard suspicion in Ellie's voice, but maybe it was his own guilt. "Really? Glad to hear he found a place then. I'd recommended a few apartments around town, but your area is the nicest."

Ellie agreed, and she was about to ask him another question about Pax when Ted's cell phone rang.

"Oh, gotta take this. Sorry, buttercup. I'll catch up with you soon." Ted left her office without another word.

Ellie thought he was a little too happy to have an excuse to leave.

The next few weeks were relatively uneventful.

Ellie had been adjusting to her new role as head of the company although she felt she'd never be totally comfortable without her dad by her side. This would always be his company. He had big shoes to fill, and honestly, she'd relied on Ted to help her muddle through. Sometimes, she'd wonder why Jacob hadn't left things to Ted. But family was family, so she sort of understood that her father had wanted her to have it.

Thankfully, the nightmares had started to subside again. She had actually been getting sleep more often than not, which was a big improvement.

Ellie had seen Pax often. Initially, she had been annoyed by her attraction to him, and although that hadn't really changed, Ellie had found comfort in their newfound friendship. She'd just need to learn to put a rein on her thoughts when he was around.

At the office, it would be all business, but once they clocked out, they'd both seem to relax. Pax was easy to talk to, so she'd briefly filled him in on her disastrous engagement to Marcus. She'd confided that she believed it was never about her but about her family's money. In fact, she'd told Pax a lot about herself over the past month or so. In turn, Pax had told her small bits about his family back in Texas—how he used to get into trouble with his brothers, Jared and Bradley, and that his little sister, Alice, thought he should settle down and give her nieces and nephews.

They would even carpool now and then.

Pax got into her Mustang and claimed to be in love.

"This is the perfect car. Any woman who owns a bad boy like this must be damn near perfect, too. You should marry me." He shot her that flirtatious grin that gave her butterflies.

She laughed back at him. "Oh, no! You just want me for my car. Been down that road once already. Never gonna happen."

She was only teasing him back, but Pax's face turned suddenly serious.

"Any man who doesn't want you for who you are is an idiot. I hope you know that, Ellie."

Ellie was confused by his change in mood. He was usually smiling and teasing with a little flirting thrown in, but now, he was serious and almost looked pained. She'd never seen this side of him.

"Thank you, Pax. I appreciate you saying so." Feeling awkward, she changed the direction of the conversation to focus on him. "So, why haven't you snatched up a Mrs. Paxton yet? Half the ladies in the office are already in love with you." She laughed as she said, "You could probably take your pick." She instantly got the impression that must not have been the right thing to say.

Pax continued to look at her with an odd expression. "I don't do relationships. It never works out well."

Feeling a little guilty, Ellie decided it was her turn to encourage him. "Someday, the right woman will stumble into your life when you least expect it, and it will all fall into place for you."

Pax continued to stare at her for a moment, and she was afraid she'd said the wrong thing yet again.

He broke the silence, "Yeah, maybe."

He didn't seemed convinced, and for some reason, her mouth wouldn't stop producing words.

"Of course it will happen! You're a great guy. You're honest, genuine, and okay, I'll admit it…sexy. You're pretty much the female dream. I'll bet she comes along sooner than you think."

Pax smirked, back to his usual flirtatious self. "You think I'm sexy?"

Ellie swatted his arm. "That would be the only thing you heard!"

By the time they pulled into the parking lot, things were back to an easy, comfortable level between them.

Pax was glad that, so far, there had been no more attempts to harm Ellie. He was pretty much always around, even when she didn't realize it. Ted's quick thinking about the upgraded security system had allowed Pax to install some extra precautions in her office, such as a hidden video feed, without her being suspicious. She'd just assumed these were company-wide changes, and she never asked him about the details.

Much to his frustration, Pax was also really enjoying spending time with Ellie. He'd find himself looking forward to being near her, and when he wasn't near her, he would be thinking about her. He'd chalked it up to the job, but he knew better. She was getting under his skin.

He thought back to that comment about her ex being an idiot. He couldn't believe he'd let himself blurt that out. If he wasn't careful, she was going to realize he cared for her. While that was okay in a friendship sort of way, he feared his feelings were starting to go deeper than that. That wasn't a complication either of them wanted or needed. She had made it clear that she wasn't interested in dating anyone despite him feeling sure she was attracted to him, and he knew that emotions only muddied up the waters in his line of work. As he'd told her before, he didn't do relationships.

Early one Friday morning, Ted called, requesting to see him as soon as possible.

Pax passed the reception desk and smiled at Christin as he headed toward Ted's office. She was usually cheerful, but this morning, she was rubbing her back and looking generally uncomfortable.

"Not long now," Pax said, hoping to encourage her.

She gave him a thumbs-up and went back to looking miserable.

Pax entered the small waiting area where he'd first met Ted and saw that Ms. Patricks was on the phone. She waved him in, indicating that Ted was already waiting for him. Behind his desk, Ted was pensive and tense.

"Tell me what happened," Pax said as he closed the office door behind him.

Ted reached out to hand him an envelope. Pax recognized the familiar handwriting and knew immediately that it was another letter from the blackmailer.

"When did this arrive?"

Ted ran his hands through his hair, disheveling his normally put-together appearance. "I guess sometime between last night and this morning. It was in the mail drop."

Pax pulled the letter out of the envelope and quickly read through it. The words swam before him as his anger began to rise. "Damn it! Ted, this is serious! He knows I'm protecting her. He's been watching us all this time!"

Pax tossed the letter on Ted's desk and let out a string of obscenities before he sat down and tried to think clearly. Ted simply looked lost.

"As I've said before, I know hiring you was the right decision. He might know why you are here, but without you, he might have already made his move. Ellie would be…" Ted couldn't finish the thought. It was too horrific.

Pax ran the threats through his mind. This person knew a lot about her—her habits, her friends, and even about her new secret bodyguard, which was something Ellie herself didn't know about. Only a sick mind would threaten to do some of the things mentioned in the letter. This time, there was no threat of exposure of past deeds or demands for money. This sicko was angry that Pax was here. It appeared to be all about revenge now. Ellie had never done anything to anyone, yet this freak had accused her of ruining his, or her, life. It simply didn't make sense to Pax.

Why is so much vehemence directed at her?

It was a frightening puzzle, and Pax needed to quickly find the pieces. There were precious few clues indicating who might be behind this, and now, Pax knew this villain was ready to strike again.

Pax grabbed the letter once again, slightly crushing it in his fist. "I'll take care of it."

Before Ted had a chance to inquire about Pax's next move, Pax was out the door and heading to the elevators. He needed to see Ellie. He needed to talk to her. Pulling out his smartphone, he opened the app connected to the video feed in her office. He could see her sitting at her desk with the phone against one ear and her other hand absentmindedly twirling a lock of hair around her fingers. He smiled despite his frustration. He realized that since meeting Ellie, he'd been smiling a lot.

"Cut it out, moron," he said to himself just before the doors opened.

When he reached her office, Ellie was just hanging up the phone and writing something on a Post-it note.

"Hey," said Pax as he knocked on her doorjamb.

She looked up at him and motioned for him to enter. "What's up?" she asked as she put some files in the cabinet below her desk.

Pax leaned his hip against one of her large padded office chairs as he said, "I was thinking we could grab pizza and a movie tonight. Ya know, just hang out. I'm tired of sitting around my apartment, watching reruns and eating frozen dinners."

Ellie looked surprised for a brief moment but recovered quickly. "Sure, that sounds fun. Any specific movie in mind?"

Pax shook his head. "I'm up for anything. I haven't seen too many in the last few years, so probably most anything will be new to me."

Ellie stuck the end of the pen in her mouth and ran through a mental list of the DVDs she owned. Pax closed his eyes. Those lips and her little harmless habits were going to be the death of him.

"Anything?" asked Ellie. "There are a few movies I've been meaning to watch, but I haven't had a chance to see them yet."

"Sounds good," said Pax. "I'll be over around six. We can order the pizza then, and I'll bring the beer."

Ellie wrinkled her nose. "Great, but don't expect me to drink beer. I'm more of a wine girl."

Pax laughed at her. "Wuss."

Ellie stuck her tongue out at him. "I'm proud of my wuss status, so bite me."

Pax had to fight the urge to say, *Don't tempt me.* Instead, he tuned on his heel and said, "See ya tonight."

Later at home, Ellie spent almost an hour figuring out what to wear. She'd first decided on jeans and a T-shirt, and then she'd thought she should wear something a little dressier. Instead, she switched to sweats and then back to jeans again. Ellie wondered why it mattered to her so much. It wasn't a date. He was a friend, and that was it. They were just hanging out. She didn't even want him to think of her that way, so she didn't understand why she was suddenly in a panic over how she looked.

Frustrated with herself, she decided her well-worn jeans would have to do. She brushed her hair out and pulled it up into a clip, and then she reapplied her lipstick and surveyed herself in the mirror.

"You're not fooling anyone, Ellie," she said to her reflection.

Trying not to be attracted to Pax was like trying not to breathe. She could only go for so long before she would find herself gasping for air.

Ellie went into the living room and started pulling out her DVDs. While setting aside a few she thought Pax might like, the doorbell rang. Answering the door, she suddenly felt a little underdressed. Pax was wearing a white button-up shirt with the top button undone. His form-fitting jeans looked brand-new, and his black boots were immaculate. All he needed was the hat, and he'd look like he'd two-stepped off the cover of a cowboy magazine.

She stepped back to allow him in, and he presented her with a bottle of Moscato. "I know it's not great with pizza, but I thought it might be nice after dinner."

Ellie smiled. Moscato was her favorite. She briefly entertained the silly notion that he had somehow known this detail, but her logic crushed that idea. It was obviously just a lucky guess. "Thank you, I love Moscato!" She motioned for him to take a seat on the sofa and said "Where's your beer? I'll put it in the fridge for you."

Pax shook his head. "I didn't bring any. I thought the wine was a better idea."

Ellie playfully pushed him aside and laughed. "Of course it was a better idea. It was my idea."

Pax plopped himself on her sofa and put his feet up on the coffee table. "Since you're so smart, I'll let you choose the pizza, too."

Ellie sat down beside him and gave him a look of teasing annoyance. "Oh, you'll let me? Thank you, your highness. Anything else I can do for you?"

Pax gave her a wide smile but didn't say a word. He didn't need to. She knew he was holding back something inappropriate. She rolled her eyes, picked up her phone, and dialed her favorite pizza place.

After ordering the pizza, they looked through several DVDs. Pax hadn't been kidding when he said most of the movies would probably be new to him. Looking around, he pointed out that she didn't have any horror movies.

Ellie's voice took on a serious tone. "I don't really like them much."

Pax wanted to kick himself. *How could I have forgotten what she'd witnessed as a girl?* She hadn't said much to him about it, but he had certainly learned enough from Ted to know that she'd struggled with it for years. Her therapist had told Jacob that she had dissociative amnesia. She couldn't remember all the details, but she remembered enough of the trauma that it haunted her.

Wanting to put a smile back on her face, Pax grabbed a chick flick off the top of the pile. "How about this one?"

Ellie incredulously looked at him. "Really? You wanna watch *While You Were Sleeping?* That's an old one, and it's pretty girlie. Think your manliness can handle it?"

Pax smiled at her as he held the DVD in front of her face. "Bring it on."

When the pizza arrived, Ellie went to the kitchen to get the plates and iced tea. Pax asked where the bathroom was, and then while she was preoccupied with the food, he took a moment to check every window in the back of the apartment. Finding them all locked securely, Pax finally felt he could relax a bit and enjoy these stolen moments with Ellie.

5

Pax sat on the couch, slowly enjoying his only glass of wine. He needed to keep a clear head, but it was becoming difficult with Ellie on her second glass and getting comfortable by his side. She had her feet curled up beneath her, and she was so close to him that their shoulders almost touched. He was having a hard time concentrating on the movie, too. It was most certainly a chick flick, and he couldn't keep up with who was actually in love with whom. When Bill Pullman's character talked to Sandra Bullock's character about leaning—where a guy leaned into a girl with the intention of being seductive—Pax chuckled out loud.

Ellie's head popped up a little straighter, and she said, "What? Is that not really a thing?"

Pax meant to tease her, so he leaned in close, practically trapping Ellie in place, similar to the way Pullman did on the screen. "It absolutely is a thing."

His teasing moment suddenly backfired. Ellie locked eyes with him, and without even realizing she was doing it, she licked her bottom lip and then drew it into her mouth. Pax was mesmerized by that one little movement. He wanted to kiss her. He wanted her more than he wanted his next breath. He started to close the gap when her phone rang and startled them both. She sprang away from him like he was on fire and jumped up to get her cell. He cursed under his breath, not sure who he was more upset with—the caller or himself.

Ellie took her cell phone into the kitchen. When she answered, Nessa was on the other end, chattering excitedly about a party. Ellie could hear the thundering bass in the background. The party scene was much more Nessa's thing than Ellie's, but occasionally, they would go out together.

"Ellie, girl! You gotta come check out this party I'm at. It's at Nate's house, and it's been a blast! Hot guys and booze everywhere!" It sounded like Nessa was already well on her way to diminishing the party's alcohol supply.

"Sorry, Nessa. I'm watching a movie tonight. But you have fun for me."

Nessa snorted sarcastically. "Seriously? You need to get out and live a little. Marcus was a douche nozzle, but that doesn't mean they all are. You need to quit spending so much time alone."

Ellie couldn't help but laugh. "I know, Nessa. Honestly, I'm enjoying a quiet night here, and I'm not alone. I'm watching with, uh…a friend."

Nessa was quiet for a moment. "Is that hunky Pax there?" When Ellie didn't reply, Nessa came to her own conclusion. "He is! He is! Oh, girl, you just stay right there. But you gotta fill me in on all the down and dirty details tomorrow, you hear me?"

Ellie sighed. "Nessa…" she warned.

She heard Nessa squeal with excitement and knew that nothing she could say would convince her friend that she wasn't on a date with Pax.

Nessa had met Pax a couple of times. The first time, she'd stopped by the apartment to see Ellie, and Nessa had met him in the hallway. Another time, he'd come into the diner.

Nessa had gone on and on about how hot he was and how she would surely tap that if Ellie wasn't going to. Of course, Nessa hadn't yet followed through on her threat, and she likely wouldn't after tonight, believing Ellie had claimed him.

"I'm hanging up, Nessa. Make sure you get a ride home."

Nessa quickly yelled back, "I want details!"

"No drunk driving!" Ellie replied before hanging up.

Ellie walked back into the living room to find Pax refilling her wine glass. She would have made a joke about him getting her drunk, but she was afraid where that might lead. It seemed like they were both saying the wrong things tonight. She accepted the glass he offered her and sat back down on the couch, a little farther away from him than before. Distance was safe. Distance was a buffer. Distance would keep her from jumping his bones before the night was over. Pax picked up the remote and restarted the movie since he'd thoughtfully paused it when she got up to answer her phone.

Pax sat through the rest of the movie, making small comments and trying to get them back to familiar ground. Ellie seemed to relax again although she was farther away from him than he would've liked. It looked like she was the smarter one after all. Despite what had almost happened, he wanted her close to him.

By the end of the movie, Ellie had dozed off in her corner of the couch. Pax turned everything off and then went into her room. He pulled the blanket off of the bed and brought it back into the living room. He covered her up and stood there, looking at her, wondering what to do next. He wasn't comfortable with leaving her alone, but he knew she wouldn't be cool with him spending the night. He had no idea how he would explain that without giving away his secret.

A lock of hair had come loose from her clip and was on her cheek. Without thinking, he reached down and gently brushed it back out of her face, tucking it behind her ear. She stirred just a little and then snuggled down more into the blanket. He couldn't help himself. He leaned in close to her face and kissed her forehead. Then, he settled into the chair next to the couch and watched her sleep.

Realization slapped him across the face like a splash of ice water. He wanted her. He wanted Elizabeth Manchester, and he didn't care if it was a bad idea. Maybe they could find a way to make it work. Maybe they could overcome the various obstacles between them. Maybe. He had to try because she was a once-in-a-lifetime girl, and he believed she was worth the effort.

As the sun began to rise, Pax quietly slipped out the door and across the hall to his own apartment. He'd catch a couple of hours of sleep and then figure out his next move. Ellie should be safe for the moment, but there was no telling what the day ahead held for either of them.

Ellie awoke to the bright sunlight shining through her living room windows. *What time is it? And why am I on my sofa?*

With dawning horror, she realized she'd had a little too much wine and dozed off, leaving poor Pax to fend for himself—not that he couldn't, but what a rude hostess she had been. She owed him an apology.

She sat up and stretched her arms and legs. Then, she realized her bedspread was around her waist. Pax must have covered her up before he'd left last night. Her heart swelled just a bit at the idea of him taking care of her. Even Marcus had never been that sweet. He would've left her cold and shivering, and he probably would have been pissed off that she'd fallen asleep to begin with.

She grabbed her blanket, shuffled into the bedroom, and tossed it back on her bed. Then, she went into the kitchen to start some coffee. She was going to need it today.

After showering, she donned a floral sundress and sandals. Then, she slipped a headband in her hair to get it out of her face. Pouring her third cup of coffee, she sat at the breakfast bar and flipped through the newspaper. There was a huge flea market in town this weekend, and she thought it might be fun to check it out. She grabbed her purse and keys and then opened her front door. Pax was standing there, his finger less than an inch from the doorbell.

"Well, that was great timing," he said, smiling. Then, he looked her over. "Whoa. Going somewhere special? You look amazing. If you have a date, I might have to kill him."

He winked, and she knew he was teasing, but her heart skipped a beat anyway.

"I'm heading to the flea market on Tenth Street. This is the only weekend it will be in town, and I love looking at all the antiques." She shut the door behind her and checked that it was locked.

Pax, looking rather nice himself in a pair of tan cargo shorts and a blue polo, scratched his head. "Antiques? I've never really been antique shopping."

Ellie smirked and said, "What? Too mature for you? Would you rather look for comic books?"

Pax pretended to be offended. "Of course I'd rather look for comic books. I'm not a heathen." He offered her his arm and said, "But I suppose I can grow up for one day, if you don't mind the company."

Ellie smirked at him. "You? Grow up? This, I have to see." She looped her arm in his.

Pax gave her one of his heart-stopping smiles. "Let's go look at antiques."

She laughed out loud. *Oh, how this man makes me smile.* If she weren't careful, Ellie could lose her heart to him without even trying.

Ten minutes later, they were pulling into a parking space at the community center. Pax had insisted on driving the Mustang, and Ellie was in a good mood, so she had been happy to let him.

Pax quickly slipped out of the driver's seat and ran around to her side of the car. He opened the door for her, and she took his offered hand. When she got out of the car, she thanked him. He was being too nice—not that she didn't like it, but she wasn't sure she should be encouraging this kind of attention. Something about it bordered on more than friendly.

Walking into the building, Pax looked around at the rows and rows of booths. The setup was like a maze. "Wow. I had no idea people would have this much crap to sell."

Ellie gave his shoulder a light smack. "You can leave, you know. You did invite yourself after all."

Pax held up a hand to block her next blow. "Hey, it's a free country."

She raised an eyebrow at him. "Really? So, if you hadn't run into me in the hall, you would have come here of your own free will?"

He pretended to think about that for a moment. "Absolutely!"

Ellie rolled her eyes. "Liar."

She walked away to look at the closest booth. He quickly caught up with her and inspected some old tools in the booth across the aisle. He surveyed the immediate area and tried to determine the layout. Keeping an eye on her and everyone else with this much stuff everywhere was going to be tricky. He concluded that his best bet would be to just stay by her side.

He walked back over to the booth where Ellie stood. She was looking closely at something she called depression glass. He had no clue what that was, but he agreed that the cobalt blue was striking. She was oohing and aahing over the patterns, but he couldn't seem to take his eyes off of her. She looked up at him and caught him staring. He cleared his throat and grabbed the first thing near him, acting as if he'd been inspecting that instead of her. Ellie giggled. He looked down to see he was holding what looked to be a very old yellowing corset.

Great. He held it up to his chest and said, "What do you think? Is it my color?"

Ellie stepped back and looked him over. "No. You'd look better in pink."

He tossed it back on the table and pretended to be insulted. "Glad to hear it."

She smiled and walked over to the next booth. Pax hoped he didn't look like a lovesick puppy following her around because he was starting to feel like one.

A couple of hours had passed, and Ellie was immensely enjoying herself. Pax was fun to be around, and he was taking all this junk shopping with grace. She suspected he was having at least a little fun as well.

Then, they found the booth with comic books. Pax appeared to be in his own personal heaven. She watched him grab various books, declaring their value based on the year, issue, or cast of characters. She had no idea they were actually collectible. It was cool to see him so passionate about the subject.

Noticing the bathroom was just around the corner from the comic merchant, she slipped away and went inside the tiny hallway. Since she'd only be gone for a few minutes, she saw no need to interrupt Pax's animated conversation with the elderly man running the booth. On the right were two doors, marked men and women, and at the end of the hall was an emergency exit. She noticed the lighted sign above the door was out.

She entered the ladies' room and took care of business. After washing her hands and exiting the restroom, she saw something out of the corner of her eye, so she turned her head. The next thing she knew, a hand was over her mouth, and she was being dragged backward and out the back door. She kicked out and struggled, but she couldn't seem to get away. She tried to bite the fingers over her mouth, but she couldn't get purchase on the flesh pressed against her lips. Ellie panicked. She attempted to scream, but most of it came out choked and muffled.

The voice of the man behind her growled, "Shut up!"

She tried to twist within his grip, hoping she could manage a kick to the groin, but she stumbled and tripped herself and the man pulling her toward his car. They both tumbled to the concrete.

As she quickly tried to get up, she heard Pax's worried shouts as he burst out the back door, "Ellie! Ellie! Where are you?"

Her masked abductor realized Pax was coming and jumped into his car. Pax saw the new red Dodge Charger peel out and take off.

Pax ran to her just in time to catch her as she fainted dead away.

Pax carried her to the Mustang, unlocked the doors, and placed her inside on the passenger seat. He crouched beside her and checked her vital signs. She seemed to be okay, other than the fainting. She must have been terrified. He also noticed blood running down her leg. Carefully lifting the hem of her dress, he saw that the fall had skinned her knees. He opened the glove box, looking for napkins or anything else to press against the scrapes and stop the bleeding. There was nothing usable in there, so he took off his shirt and pressed it against the knee bleeding the worst.

It must have hurt because Ellie's eyes flew open. "Damn!" she cried out.

Pax grabbed her face and made her focus on him. "Are you okay? Are you hurt anywhere else?"

She slightly shook her head and then winced. "I think I might have sprained my ankle."

Pax cautiously touched the ankle that was starting to look a little puffy. He nodded his head in agreement. "Let's get you home."

He carefully shut her door, then he sprinted over to pick up her dropped purse. After returning to the car and climbing into the driver's side, he started the engine and pulled out into traffic. He was anything but calm. He wanted to chase down the bastard who had attacked her and beat him until his ancestors felt it. But right now, he had to focus on her. She was hurt.

"Do you want to go to the hospital? We could have that ankle x-rayed."

She shook her head, and Pax could see tears forming in her eyes. He wanted to hold her. He wanted to kill someone. He wanted…he wanted things he couldn't have. He'd let his guard down, and she'd gotten hurt. He was angry, mostly with himself. This was why he could never let emotions get in the way. They clouded good judgment, and the client paid the price.

Once they were home, he came around to her side and helped her out of the car. She attempted to put her weight on her right ankle, but even though she could stand, he could tell it was uncomfortable. Without even asking, he scooped her up into his arms and carried her up to her apartment. He took the key from her and opened the door. He entered and then kicked it shut behind him. Without stopping, he headed straight for her bedroom. She started to protest, but something about his expression warned her to stay quiet. Pax looked like he was on the warpath.

Laying her on the bed, Pax disappeared into her bathroom for a few moments. Then, he reappeared holding a wet washcloth, antibiotic ointment, and a box of bandages. Ellie pulled herself up to a sitting position as Pax sat on the bed next to her. He carefully cleaned her knees and wiped the blood off her calves. Then, he went to work putting antibiotic on the scrapes. Once cleaned up, they weren't really all that bad. It took only a couple of small bandages to cover them up. Pax then began to inspect her ankle. She tried to wiggle it a bit, but it hurt. She held in a groan, and Pax frowned even more.

"You'll need to stay off of that for a couple of days," he said decisively.

Ellie didn't answer. She only stared down at her ankle, wondering how such a beautiful day had gone so terribly wrong.

Pax went to the kitchen to make an ice pack. He heard Ellie's phone ringing in her purse, so he grabbed it and headed back to her bedroom. Handing the cell to Ellie, he started placing pillows under her foot to elevate it, and then he placed the ice pack on her ankle. She glanced at the ringing phone and tossed it aside. She wasn't in the mood for Nessa's questions right now. Closing her eyes, she leaned her head back.

When she opened them again, Pax was sitting next to her, still looking angry. She reached out to him, and he flinched.

"Pax?"

He stood up and paced the room. "I was looking at comic books. Stupid-ass comic books! I should have been with you. Where did you go?" he roared.

She was taken aback by just how furious he was. *Is he mad at me?* That made no sense. "I went to the restroom. It was right around the corner. I hadn't expected that some dirtbag was going to grab me on the way back."

Pax turned and glared at her. "You couldn't tell me where you were going? You had to just disappear without a word? What are you? Five?"

He is mad at me! He is accusing me as if it were my fault this had happened!

She yelled back at him, "No, actually, I'm not five, which is why I don't need a damn babysitter, and I decided to go without your permission!" Determined not to listen to any more of his nonsense, she tossed the ice pack across the room and got off the bed.

Pax started toward her. "Sit your ass back down!"

She defiantly lifted her chin. "I'm not spending another minute in this room with you, you...pompous jackass!" Then, she hobbled toward the bedroom door.

Pax was instantly at her side and blocked her passage out of the room. "I said, get back on that bed." His voice was now calm, but it had an edge to it that told her he was struggling to restrain himself.

Turning to face him fully, she blurted out, "Screw you!"

A little too late, Ellie realized that had been the wrong answer. Pax braced his arms on either side of the bedroom door and trapped her against it. He looked into her eyes for a moment, and she registered a deep emotion there—fear mingled with something else she couldn't put her finger on. Then, suddenly, he had her pressed up against the door, his body pinning her, and he was kissing her with a fierceness that had caught her completely off guard. Pax's hands went to both sides of her face, and he buried his fingers in her hair.

She couldn't believe this was happening. She couldn't breathe. She couldn't help but kiss him back, and she felt like she'd never be able to stop. Her hands roamed his bare chest, and he pulled away from her lips long enough to tilt her head to one side, giving him access to her neck. She moaned, and Pax smiled between kisses, slowly working his way to her collarbone. He slid one strap of her sundress off her shoulder and started kissing there, too.

This was about the time Ellie's brain began to function again. No, they couldn't do this. She couldn't do this. She pushed him away although she wasn't sure he'd even noticed her effort at first. Pax pulled away just enough to look at her face, but most of his body was still pressing her against the door.

Ellie cleared her throat as she pulled the strap of her dress back up. She shook her head. "Pax, what's going on here? What are we doing?"

Pax refused to move away from her even though she would have appreciated some extra space at that moment. He still needed to touch her, so he could assure himself that she was there with him, and she was safe. All he could think about was the fear he'd felt when he turned around in that flea market, and she was gone. He'd quickly walked up and down a couple of different aisles, but it hadn't taken him long to realize something wasn't right.

If I hadn't reached her when I did…

What if that guy would have successfully dragged her into his car? I might have never found her.

He shuddered at the thought.

She continued to look at him with the question hanging between them. He wanted to say something ridiculous, something she'd expect him to say to lighten the mood. But he couldn't. It was time to be serious.

"I don't really know what's happening between us, Ellie. It's as much a mystery to me as it is to you. But I do know that it feels right. You feel right."

Ellie closed her eyes. "Pax, we've talked about our epic fails in the relationship department. Regardless of how this feels, it's not right. We're just running on adrenaline. We'll wake up tomorrow, hating ourselves—or worse, each other—if we go through with this."

Pax took a step back. He knew she was right. There could never be anything between them. He tried to convince himself that it was probably just lust anyway. What he didn't understand was why he felt like she had just shoved a dagger into his heart. He nodded his head and backed out of the bedroom a few steps. Then, he turned around and walked toward the front door, digging his keys out of his pocket. Ellie wasn't sure where he was going or if she should even try to stop him.

Pax pulled open the door and then turned to look at her. "You should sit down. That ankle might not be sprained, but it would probably be good to stay off of it as much as possible, just in case." Then, he jerked his head toward his apartment. "I'll be back in a moment. I need a new shirt." And with that, he was gone.

6

Ellie found the ice pack near the window and picked it up. She grabbed her phone off the bed and then slowly made her way into the living room. Sitting in the armchair, she put her foot up on the coffee table and applied the ice pack to her ankle once more. After listening to the voice mail Nessa had left her, Ellie's suspicions were confirmed. Nessa was demanding details about a date that had never happened. There was no way in hell Ellie was going to tell her about the encounter up against the bedroom door even if it was the hottest thing she'd ever experienced in her life.

Pax knocked, and without waiting for her reply, he entered the apartment. He had on a fresh white T-shirt and had changed into jeans. His expression was now all business. Ellie found herself disappointed that he could get over their kisses so quickly when she was still reeling from it all.

She mentally slapped herself. *Idiot.*

This was what they both needed to do, so it was necessary that she move on as well. However, she knew she'd never again view her bedroom door without reliving their encounter.

Pax watched Ellie fiddle with her phone. She seemed calm and collected. He was glad to see she'd taken his words to heart and had at least sat down. He would figure out how to deal with the emotional complications later, but right now, he had to find out who her attacker was. He poured them both a glass of tea and brought them into the living room.

Handing her one of the drinks, Pax sat on the end of the sofa closest to the armchair. "I need to ask you some questions. Are you up for it?"

Ellie nodded, but she was hoping he wouldn't want to talk about what had just happened between them.

Pax cleared his throat again, and she could see him struggling to keep his calm.

Then, he looked at her and said, "Did you recognize anything about your attacker or his car?"

Ellie stopped with the tea glass midway to her lips. *My attacker? How could I have forgotten about that so easily?* Well, she hadn't really forgotten, but she sure hadn't been thinking about him a few minutes ago. Attempting to focus, she tried to remember every detail, but nothing really stood out.

"No, I don't think I knew him. I'm not sure about the car since I kinda fainted before I got a good look."

Pax nodded in understanding. "Did he say anything to you?"

Ellie shook her head, only to quickly correct herself. "Well, he did tell me to shut up when I tried to scream, but I didn't recognize the voice. It was rough, almost like he was trying to disguise it."

Pax leaned back on the couch and ran a hand over his face. Ellie thought he looked tired and frustrated. Then, it hit her that something was off about all of this.

Why did someone try to take me? Did I look like an easy target? Was I unfortunate enough to be in the wrong place at the wrong time, so he took a chance that he could get away with me?

For a moment, Ted's words about her being in danger popped into her mind, but she brushed that away. Ted hadn't said any more about it, and there was no real reason to believe she'd been the intended target—unless maybe someone was hoping to get ransom in exchange for her. That was always a possibility.

"Pax, why do you think he grabbed me?"

Pax sat up and clasped his hands together. At first, she wasn't sure he was going to answer her.

After a thoughtful moment, he said, "I'm not sure. Could be a number of reasons."

Ellie nodded, but she felt like he wasn't telling her something. Maybe she was just tired.

Pax stood up. "If you don't need anything else right now, I have a couple of things to take care of. We also need to call the police and report what happened."

The last thing Ellie felt like doing was talking to the police, but she knew Pax was right. "Sure, I'm good for now. But do you think we can put off calling the police until tomorrow?"

Pax shook his head. "We really need to talk to them while the details are fresh. The longer we wait, the harder it'll be to find this dirtbag."

Ellie nodded in understanding. "Okay. Call them."

Two hours later, Ellie and Pax had given their statements to the police, and she was resting in her room. Pax was pacing the living room, trying to figure out his next move. He hated lying to Ellie. He needed to convince Ted to let him tell her the truth. She might be safer if she understood the seriousness of the situation. Pax peeked in on Ellie and found her fast asleep. He quietly slipped out of her apartment and pulled out his cell phone.

Ted answered after two rings.

"Ted, it's Pax. We really need to tell Ellie about the letters."

Ted could sense the urgency in Pax's voice. "What happened? Was she attacked again?"

Pax couldn't help but feel the anger starting to bubble up inside him all over again. "Yes, someone tried to kidnap her. She managed to trip him and slow him down long enough for me to get there. Then, he ran."

Ted asked for details, so Pax filled him in.

"We've filed a police report, but we have to tell Ellie what's going on. She deserves to know."

Ted disagreed. "Pax, if we tell her, she'll just worry. If she continues to think this was a random attack, she can go on feeling like her life is normal."

Pax didn't like it one bit.

Ted continued, "It's all Ellie has left, Pax. She values control and normality more than anything else. If we take that away from her, she'll crumble. We need to figure this out and eliminate the threat. She never needs to know. Besides, I still don't have any answers about her dad and the blackmail situation. I can't tarnish him in her eyes in any way. I refuse to do that to her."

Pax sighed loudly. "All right. You know her better than I do. I wouldn't dream of hurting her, so I'll trust you on this."

"Thanks Pax. I'll stop by and check on her later today."

Pax hung up, pushed the cell in his pocket and went back inside Ellie's apartment. He'd wait to see how her ankle was holding up after she woke up. By then, the ibuprofen should have kicked in. She might need his assistance for a while. He was glad to help, but he knew it was going to be damn hard to keep his hands off of her. He envisioned a lot of cold showers in his future.

Pax locked the door behind him and made himself comfortable on the sofa. He quickly dozed off.

He had been asleep for about half an hour when he heard something that didn't sound right. He bolted upright, slightly disoriented. After getting his bearings, he sat still, trying to figure out what it was that had awoken him. All was quiet for a moment, but then he heard it again. *Moaning? Crying? Both?*

Pax made a mad dash for Ellie's room.

Throwing open the door, he saw Ellie thrashing under the covers, mumbling something about her father. Then, he caught the word *mommy* and heard Ellie cry. He sat next to her, toward the head of her bed, and tried to gently wake her, but she was firmly entrenched in her nightmare. She was still crying although somewhat silently. Pax wasn't sure what to do, but he knew he couldn't leave her like this. Following his instinct, he climbed in bed with her and pulled her to him. She seemed to resist a bit at first, but she quickly relaxed and curled into the comfort of his arms. Her cries became sniffles, and then her breathing eventually slowed down to a normal pace before she was sleeping soundly again.

Pax couldn't have moved if he'd wanted to. Obviously, this wasn't the way to keep a professional distance from her, but he couldn't stand to see her in pain. He was determined to give her whatever she needed to rest even if she wouldn't remember it. Pax held her for quite a while, mostly because he could, until he heard a knock on the door.

Carefully getting up, he straightened his clothing and checked the peephole. Ted stood on the other side with a small bouquet of daisies in hand. Pax opened the door. "Hi Ted. Come on in."

Pax took the flowers and searched for a vase. After finding one under the kitchen sink, he placed the daisies inside with some water and put them on the counter.

Ted took a seat in the armchair. "I just came to see how my girl was. Is she asleep?"

"Yeah, she's had a rough day," Pax said as he situated himself on the arm of the sofa. He glanced at Ted and furrowed his brow. "Did you know that she's having nightmares? Is this something she deals with often?"

Ted frowned. "Hell. I knew she used to, but I thought they had stopped recently."

Pax sighed. "Well, they must be back. Maybe today's trauma had set them off. I don't think I've ever seen someone so tortured during sleep."

Ted put his head in his hands. "Despite years of therapy, I don't think she's ever come to grips with all the tragedy in her life. I can't even imagine what that poor girl is going through, and I loved her family, too."

Pax stared down at the floor, trying to imagine a young Ellie fighting to handle the terror like an adult. "I'm not sure anyone could get over something like that, not completely, but she's strong, stronger than almost anyone I know."

Ted nodded in agreement.

Ellie slept for several more hours.

Ted had left, but not before asking Pax to let her know he'd stopped by.

Pax searched the hall closet and found an extra blanket. Then, he made himself comfortable on the sofa once more. One way or another, he was going to make sure he was there for Ellie even if that meant camping in her living room and annoying the hell out of her.

Three days later, Ellie was able to walk almost normally although she wouldn't be running any marathons for a while. Pax had been a constant companion despite her protests. He had been sweet and caring, but also frustrating and bullheaded. She, on the other hand, had felt confused and angry.

Thankfully, Pax could go about his regular schedule now that she wasn't quite so handicapped. She knew Ted wouldn't fire Pax since he had been helping her out, but he was needed at the company, and she was ready to get back to her normal routine as well. It was discomfiting to have things so out of whack. It was another reminder of the chaos that had infested her life as of late.

Ellie had worked from home the day before, but today, she was going back to the office. Pax insisted on driving her to work even though she felt well enough to drive on her own. She wasn't interested in arguing with Pax, which was kind of unusual for her. She didn't normally let anyone tell her what to do, but after the kiss in her bedroom, she wasn't sure a confrontation with him would be the best idea. She needed a better handle on her own feelings before she could take on that task.

Pax wasn't happy about her going back to work just yet, but Ellie had been persistent. Pax was determined to be near her every moment he could.

He walked her to her office, saying he wanted to be sure her ankle held out. Once inside, she went to the window to gaze out at the complex for a moment. Pax tried not to stare, but she truly was mesmerizing. The light shone on her hair, giving it almost fiery red highlights. Her creamy porcelain skin looked like it glowed. In that moment, he was sure she was an angel. He didn't deserve an angel, and God knew she deserved better than him, but there was no doubt that he'd die protecting her if necessary.

Ellie expelled a soft sigh, and Pax realized she must be lost in thought. She turned and seemed surprised that Pax was still there.

"Sorry. I guess I was woolgathering. Do you need something before I start my day?"

Pax moved toward her, his expressive blue eyes locked on her face. She wondered if he was going to try to kiss her again. She also wondered if she'd have the fortitude to tell him no. Instead of leaning in for a kiss, he stopped just in front of her and reached for her hands. His touch was warm and sent tingly sensations up her arms. She tried to calm her racing heart.

Pax inspected the hands before him and then looked into her eyes. He knew it was a bad idea, but he just needed to kiss this angel one more time. He pulled her toward him to close the short gap between them, and then he placed a gentle kiss on her lips.

"Have a good day, Ellie. Be safe. I'll see you after work." He turned and left the room before he could do something they'd both regret.

Ellie watched Pax leave and then sat at her desk. She brought her fingers up to her lips as she tried to understand what that kiss had been about. It wasn't passion-filled but more caring and maybe even loving. She giggled at her ridiculous thoughts. Of course it was caring. Despite their attraction, they were friends. Even though they'd never sleep together or be a couple, it didn't mean that they couldn't show friendly affection. She could tell that Pax had been worried about her. He was just a friend concerned about a friend. It couldn't possibly be more because that would make this situation all the more tragic. Surely, life couldn't be that cruel, even to her.

Pax was waiting in the lobby when Ellie walked out of the elevator. Leaning against the reception counter, he was talking with Christin and two of the company accountants, Robert and Tara. While Ellie generally got along with everyone in the company, Tara was not one of her favorite people. She was catty and snotty, and she had always looked down on Ellie, even when they were kids.

Tara was a classic beauty with blonde hair, blue eyes, and legs that went on forever. She had won local and state beauty pageants, and at one time, she had been expected to be a Miss America contestant. Much to her dismay, she had lost that spot to a girl from Tulsa, and she hadn't taken that well at all. She simply wasn't a nice person.

Ellie steeled herself for any subtle but venom-filled jabs that Tara might spew her way, and she started toward the group. Tara caught Ellie watching them and formed her mouth into a smirk before taking a step closer to Pax and placing a hand on his arm. Then, she leaned forward and whispered something in his ear that made them both laugh. Ellie felt jealousy bubbling up from somewhere deep within. She had no doubt that had been Tara's intention. At the very least, Tara was trying to lay some kind of claim on him.

Pax noticed Ellie heading toward them, and he excused himself from the group.

Tara reluctantly let go of his arm. "But we were gonna go have a drink! Won't you join us? It won't be as fun without you, Tanner." Then, Tara maneuvered those full lips into her trademark pout that usually preceded her getting her way.

This only served to irritate Ellie further.

Pax politely declined the invitation, but he gave Tara his most charming smile. "Maybe some other time." As he walked in Ellie's direction, he asked, "Ready to go?"

Ellie glanced over at Tara, who was still watching them, and she gave him an annoyed look. "I don't know. Are you? Or would you prefer I find another ride home, so you can go out on your date?"

Pax glanced back at the group behind him and made a disgusted face. "Believe me, I want to have a drink with her about as much as I want the clap."

Ellie couldn't help but grin. "Knowing her, you'd likely end up with both."

Pax gaped at Ellie and then busted out laughing. "Not nice, Ellie, but funny as hell."

He walked her to his Jeep and helped her in. The drive home was quiet, and he was afraid she'd pushed herself too hard today. They pulled into the parking lot of the apartment complex, and he turned off the vehicle.

Turning to face her, he said, "You okay?"

Ellie wasn't sure how to answer that. She didn't feel okay. She felt like her world was spinning off its axis. Her family was gone. She'd been attacked. And now, she was feeling jealousy over someone who shouldn't mean so much to her. Ellie nodded, but she was afraid to speak. If she opened her mouth, she might say things she could never take back, things she didn't even understand herself.

She opened the Jeep door, and as quickly as she could hobble, she went inside the building with Pax following close behind.

After unlocking her apartment door, she turned to face him again. "I'm really tired. I think I'm just gonna go to bed."

Pax's worried face almost broke her. "Are you sure? I could make us some dinner."

She fought back the tears that threatened to fall, closed her eyes, and shook her head. "I just want to sleep, but thanks."

Pax didn't appear to buy it, but she knew he wouldn't push her.

"Okay then. See you in the morning. Sleep well."

She gave him a weak smile and then stepped inside. Locking the door, she listened for Pax as he entered his own apartment and shut the door. The moment she heard his door latch, she slid down to the floor and sobbed.

7

Ellie had all but given up on a decent night's sleep. If it wasn't nightmares haunting her, it was thoughts of Pax. She needed to keep her distance. It seemed to be the only rational way to handle her attraction to him.

By their own admission, neither of them was relationship material. Ellie wasn't sure she could have a casual fling without involving her heart, especially with Pax. She feared she might be half in love with him already. The last thing she needed to add to her index of misfortune would be a massive broken heart.

Much to Pax's noticeable disappointment, she did her best to stay away from him. Working together made it difficult, but after work hours, she could generally find a way to avoid him even if that meant making up plans she didn't actually have.

A couple of weeks after the incident with Tara, Ellie was sitting on her sofa, trying to read a book. In reality, she was so lost in her thoughts about Pax that she'd barely read a word. She missed him more than she'd thought was possible. He had quickly become one of her best friends. She missed the stupid conversations they'd had. She missed his above average cooking skills. She even missed his sexy smile and ridiculous flirting, which was part of the reason she was avoiding him in the first place.

Why did life have to be so complicated?

A knock on the door jarred her out of her somewhat sullen contemplation. She pulled open the door to find Nessa on the other side, holding two bottles of wine and a brown paper sack. She pushed her way in and went straight to the kitchen. Ellie closed the door behind her and watched as Nessa dug spoons out of a drawer and pulled several pints of Ben & Jerry's out of the sack. After placing all but two pints of ice cream in the freezer, she brought the spoons and ice cream into the living room.

Nessa plopped herself on the sofa and pointed a spoon at Ellie. "Sit."

Ellie rolled her eyes and sat next to her.

Nessa handed Ellie a pint of ice cream and said, "Mint Chocolate Cookie—your favorite."

Ellie took the spoon, and following Nessa's lead, she dug into her pint. She smiled as the ice cream melted on her tongue.

"Now," said Nessa, "why don't you tell me what the hell is going on."

Ellie looked at her with innocent wide eyes. "What do you mean?"

Nessa shook her head after spooning a large bite of ice cream into her mouth. "Oh no, you don't. I know something is up. You've been hiding out in this apartment for the last couple of weeks as if you were in quarantine. You never want to have fun with me anymore."

Ellie felt bad that she'd not made time for Nessa lately, but so much had been going on, and she wasn't ready to discuss it. She didn't know what she'd even tell her friend at this point. It was all so confusing.

"I'm sorry. Life has just been crazy for me lately. I need things to calm down. After the attack at the flea market, I haven't quite been the same."

Nessa reached across to clasp Ellie's hand in hers. "Sweetie, I understand. I don't know why life continues to kick you in the balls, but I'm always here, no matter how bad it gets. Please don't block me out."

Ellie nodded and gave her a hug. Nessa smiled, leaned back, and continued to work on her ice cream.

She took a sidelong glance at Ellie and said, "At least tell me you've been spending more time with Pax. I'd gladly sacrifice some of our girl time if it meant you were getting laid again."

Ellie choked on her ice cream. "Nessa!"

"What? You can't tell me you haven't at least thought about it. Has he made a move yet?" Nessa playfully nudged Ellie with her elbow.

Looking down, Ellie pretended she hadn't heard Nessa.

"Holy crap! He did!" Tossing her almost empty container onto the coffee table, Nessa licked her spoon and turned to face Ellie, tucking one leg up underneath the other. "Details, girlie. Details!"

Ellie shook her head. "I can't talk about Pax. I can't talk about anything right now. It's just too difficult."

Ellie's sorrowful expression told Nessa all she needed to know.

Nessa gave Ellie a smile and then reached over and squeezed her hand. "It's okay, sweetie. We have ice cream, wine, and reality TV. We don't need to talk at all. Tomorrow is Saturday, and neither of us has to work, so we'll spend tonight getting fat and drunk while mocking other people's crappy lives."

Ellie laughed and was grateful that Nessa understood. Getting comfortable once again, they spent the rest of the evening watching bad television and emptying the wine bottles.

Across the hall, Pax was fuming and more than a little worried. If Ellie was going to push him away, he would have to find other means of assuring her safety. He still wasn't sure what had happened to make her withdraw from him, but it most certainly complicated things. More than once, he'd had to stop himself from breaking down her door and demanding to know why she was upset with him. But he knew that Ellie had baggage he'd likely never understand. He hated every moment away from her, but she needed space, so he'd give her space. He just had to find a way to do that and still protect her.

Saturday morning, Ellie was sipping a cup of coffee and trying to decide what to do with herself. She couldn't continue to hide in her apartment. Summer was nearing an end, and she wanted to get out and enjoy the sunshine before the cold Oklahoma winds took over.

It was already warm out, so Ellie decided to take advantage of the outdoor pool. She put on her favorite bikini, grabbed a towel, sunscreen, and a book, and then she left her apartment.

The pool was empty, for which she was eternally grateful. She enjoyed swimming laps, and it was difficult to give it her all with others in the water. Setting her stuff on a chair, she slipped off her flip-flops and lathered on some sunblock. Walking to the deep end of the pool, she wasted no time, and she dived in.

Ellie swam several laps and enjoyed the invigorating water. On her last lap, she came up for air to find Pax standing near the opposite end, watching her. He was wearing swim trunks that fit him a little too well, and she found herself imagining what he'd look like without them. Irritated that one look at his shirtless body could turn her into a blathering idiot, she swam to the ladder and climbed out.

Pax had rehearsed what he was going to say to her. Seeing her heading toward the pool, he'd quickly changed and thought about his next move. He'd watched her swim several laps before deciding to make himself known. But once she'd climbed out of the pool, he had found he couldn't speak as his mouth had suddenly gone dry.

Her green bikini had a gold ring separating the two pieces of material covering her breasts as well as gold rings on the sides of her hips that connected the front and back panels of the bottom half. She was dripping wet, and her long hair was stuck to her back and shoulders. It was the sexiest thing he'd ever seen, and he was hoping it wasn't overtly obvious because his trunks were kind of tight.

He cleared his throat. "Good morning, Ellie."

She smiled. "Good morning, Pax. Beautiful day, huh?"

"Absolutely gorgeous." Pax wasn't really talking about the day, but she could interpret that however she liked.

Ellie put on her sunglasses, stretched out on a lounge chair, and draped her arms behind her over the back of the chair. Pax wondered if she was intentionally trying to torture him. Deciding he needed a distraction, he dived into the deep end, hoping the pool water would be sufficient to cool his ardor.

Ellie watched Pax swim a few laps while she wondered how to get upstairs without looking like a coward. A fully clothed Pax was difficult enough to get out of her mind, but this was too much. She wrapped her towel around herself and slipped on her flip-flops just as Pax was exiting the pool.

"Hey, Ellie. Can I talk to you for a minute?"

He walked toward her, all wet and muscular and perfect. At that moment, she wasn't sure if she could deny him anything. She nodded and pulled her towel a little more securely around her chest.

Standing in front of her, Pax said, "I need help. I'm looking for a gift for my new niece. She's only about a week old. I know pretty much nothing about babies."

Ellie smiled despite herself. The thought of Pax picking out a girlie baby gift was something she couldn't envision. "You think I do?"

Pax's voice was almost pleading. "I don't know! I'm just totally lost on this baby stuff. Would you help me find something? Please?"

She surprised herself by saying, "Sure. When do you want to go?" She groaned inwardly. *So much for keeping my distance.*

Pax looked genuinely relieved. "This afternoon would be great, if you have the time."

Ellie suspected Pax knew she had the time. He seemed to have a talent for being around when she wasn't busy.

Pax gave her one of his classic sexy grins. "I'll even spring for lunch. Any place you want."

Ellie couldn't bring herself to turn him down.

Two hours later, they were sitting across from each other at Mattie's, discussing Pax's apartment. He had asked Ellie's advice on making it feel more like home. He wasn't the decorating type, and she had a knack for making her place comfortable. Enjoying the Saturday special of pork chops, green beans, and fry bread, she considered his request. "What kind of look are you going for? What is your style?"

Pax forked a bite of pork chop into his mouth and chewed for a moment. "Style? No idea. Something masculine, I guess. I've not stayed anywhere long enough to decorate a bachelor pad. What should it look like?"

Ellie laughed. "How should I know?" She pretended to think for a moment while chewing a bite of fry bread. "I guess you need a neon beer sign, a basketball hoop laundry hamper, and maybe some of those ugly hula girl lamps."

Pax threw a green bean at her. "I said bachelor pad, not drunken frat house."

Ellie laughed and started to toss the bean back at him when she froze. Marcus was heading toward them, and he didn't look happy. Pax turned to see what had caught her attention just as Marcus reached the table.

"Hello, Elizabeth." Marcus made an obvious show of looking her over before saying, "You look great. How have you been?"

Pax realized he was clenching his fists under the table. He didn't like the way this guy was looking at her, and Ellie sure didn't seem happy to see him.

"Hello, Marcus. I'd like to introduce you to Tanner Paxton."

Pax nodded, but he didn't attempt to shake this man's hands for fear of strangling him. This was the idiot who had given up a future with Ellie. He'd hurt her. He didn't deserve to breathe the same air as her.

Marcus gave Pax a condescending look. "Hello." he said curtly. He acted as if the very word had put a bad taste in his mouth.

Pax was pretty sure he could snap Marcus's pansy little neck, and no one would care. He continued to ball his hands into fists until his fingernails were leaving marks. As much as he'd like to break Marcus's nose, Ellie didn't need the drama.

"What do you want, Marcus?" Ellie asked in an annoyed tone.

Marcus clutched his heart as if she'd just broken it. "Why are you so unhappy to see me, sweetheart? I thought we were friends."

Ellie's mouth formed a tight line. "Marcus, I told you never to call me that again. We have nothing to talk about, so I think you should move along."

Marcus continued to push the issue, "Ellie, we have so much to talk about." With a glance at Pax, he added, "It's time we talk about us. This breakup business has gone on long enough."

Ellie seethed, "Marcus, there will never, ever be an *us* again. I don't know why you can't grasp that. Stay away from me."

Pax stood up, towering over Marcus a good four inches, and gave him a steely glare. "The lady would like for you to leave her alone. I'd advise you do just that."

Marcus turned slightly pale and then took a step back. "I know you miss me, Elizabeth. You still love me. You just won't admit it to yourself."

Then, he turned and quickly left the diner before Pax would get the chance to drag him out to the parking lot.

They finished their meals, mostly in silence, and Pax paid the check.

They went to a large retail baby store, but everything there seemed impersonal. Pax didn't know what he wanted, but he knew it had to be special. It took a little time, but once Ellie got into full shopping mode, she seemed to relax again. Walking down Main Street, they came upon a small local business full of custom-made items, and Ellie recommended a blanket embroidered with his niece's name.

"That's perfect! See? I knew you'd be a big help," said Pax.

He placed his order for a small pink-and-purple patchwork quilt with the name *Darlene* embroidered on it. As Ellie watched him pick out fabrics and thread colors for this little bundle of joy, the wall around her heart cracked just a little more.

Next, Pax drove to Pier 1 Imports and put his Jeep in park. "Are you really okay with this, too? I don't want to impose."

Ellie hated to admit it, but she was having fun, and she couldn't wait to see what kind of awful stuff he might choose. She assured him it was fine, and they went inside. He showed her the things he liked, and Ellie was surprised to learn that he actually had very good taste. They managed to find several things that would brighten up his apartment. Pax had noticed Ellie inspecting a beautiful silver mantel clock and had secretly instructed the salesclerk to add it to his purchases. Once it was all bagged up, they hauled everything to the Jeep and headed home.

A few vehicles behind them, a large man was talking on a cell phone. "Yes, sir. I'm following them now. He never seems to leave her side." A moment of silence followed, and then he replied, "Of course, sir. I'll keep you posted." He hung up the phone as he continued to follow them home.

After setting things up in his apartment, Pax walked Ellie to her door. "Thanks so much for everything today. Shopping by myself would have been a disaster. Can I make you dinner later as a thank-you?"

Ellie hesitated.

Pax pushed on, "I promise not to waste your whole night, and I'll even do the dishes afterward."

Ellie couldn't help herself. She sighed. "Fine, if it makes you feel any better, but you really don't have to."

Pax gave her a smile that didn't quite reach his eyes. "Honestly, it's my pleasure."

Later that evening, Pax went to Ellie's apartment with a bottle of wine, a sack full of groceries, and a beautifully wrapped box. He prepared a delicious lasagna, complete with caprese salad and French bread. They enjoyed the meal and kept the conversation light.

After dinner, Pax presented Ellie with the gift he'd bought her. She opened the box, and she was surprised to find the mantel clock she'd admired earlier in the day. What she didn't know was that this gift had come with strings. Pax had inserted a tiny security camera inside the clock, so he could keep tabs on her in those moments when she wouldn't want him hanging around in her apartment.

Ellie loved the clock. "Wow. Pax, you didn't have to. I mean, I love it. Don't get me wrong. But it's so expensive. You really shouldn't have."

Pax took one of her hands in his. "I wanted to, Ellie. Despite how crazy things have been between us, you've been a good friend to me. That means a lot."

Ellie felt slightly guilty. She hadn't been much of a friend lately, mostly because she couldn't keep herself from thinking about him in a more than friendly way. But that was hardly Pax's fault.

"Thank you, Pax. I love it." She placed it on the mantel above her fireplace and adjusted it, so it faced the sofa.

"You're very welcome," he said with all sincerity.

The smile she gave Pax caused his heart to skip a bit. He was happy that she loved the clock, and he was also thankful she'd put it on the mantel, which was the perfect place for the best view of the living room. It didn't cover the entire apartment, but it was better than nothing.

It was getting late, so Pax turned to leave. 'Have a good night Ellie. Don't forget to lock up."

She smiled as he slipped out of the door, touched once again by his concern for her safety. "Good night Pax."

Once inside his apartment, he made sure the video feed from the clock was working. He felt a bit like a voyeur, but he had to have some way to check on her. No one had tried anything at the apartment so far, but he wasn't going to take any chances.

For a while, she sat on the couch, reading. Then, she got up and went toward the bedroom.

Moments later, she walked back into view of the camera. Ellie had a toothbrush in one hand and seemed to be looking for something. Pax groaned. He should have known this would be difficult. Ellie was obviously getting ready for bed, and she was wearing only a tank top and panties.

How can I watch her and not watch her at the same time?

He didn't want to invade her privacy, yet doing so could mean the difference between life and death. Trying to be a gentleman, he spun his chair around, away from his computer screen. He dearly hoped she would go to bed soon because he wasn't sure how long he could remain a gentleman.

8

Pax was encouraged by the progress he'd made with Ellie so far. It had only been a few days since their shopping excursion, but she had opened up a bit more, and she hadn't given him the brush-off as often.

When she had made the excuse of being too tired to hang out, he would pretend to understand, and then he would spend the evening observing her from the clock cam. Most of the time, she would read or watch TV. While he certainly didn't mind looking at Ellie all evening, even he had his limits. He was going stir-crazy, and he wanted to be over there, within touching distance.

"Wow, Paxton," he said aloud to himself. "You really need to get your act together. You can't keep losing your mind over the client."

The problem was that she didn't feel like the client any more. He couldn't stay detached where Ellie was concerned. She was a friend, and she had become very important to him, but emotions could make him sloppy. Pax knew if he wasn't careful, his growing infatuation could get them both hurt—or worse.

After taking a quick shower and throwing on some sweats, Pax was prepared to sit at the computer, watch the Ellie show, and eat leftovers. All in all, it wasn't the worst way to do a stakeout. At least he wasn't in a cramped car. Pax had just grabbed a beer when he saw Nessa walking into Ellie's living room. Both ladies were dressed up, and they looked ready to hit the town.

"Well, looks like we are going out tonight," Pax muttered as he rushed into his bedroom to change.

Since he didn't know where they were going, he'd have to improvise to be sure he would blend in. Putting on his nicest jeans, a black button-up shirt with the sleeves rolled up, and a pair of black boots, Pax mentally prepared for the night ahead.

Nessa and Ellie spent most of the night at a club called Bones. It was a little more techno than Ellie was used to, but she was having fun.

Nessa spent a lot of time on the dance floor with a guy named Cain. Ellie had seen him around, but she didn't know him very well. He was ruggedly handsome and didn't talk about himself much. The ladies apparently loved all his mystery because he drew them in like flies. Nessa seemed to know him pretty well though, judging by how close they were dancing, which surprised Ellie.

To be totally fair, Ellie hadn't exactly been the best confidant lately. She would have to be patient and let Nessa talk about Cain on her own time and terms, if there was even anything to talk about.

Ellie asked the bartender for a rum and Coke when she felt someone slide up beside her on the barstool. She turned to see if she knew the person, but he didn't look familiar at all. He looked like he might be a college student. He was kind of cute with his wavy blond hair and soft pale blue eyes. He had to be all of twenty-four tops. She gave him a polite smile and turned back around. To her surprise, he tapped her on the shoulder, so she turned back to him, and he smiled.

"Hey, pretty lady. Don't tell me your boyfriend is out on the dance floor and left you behind. That's just criminal."

Ellie let out a giggle and shook her head. "No, nothing like that. I'm just here with my best friend to have a drink and relax."

His young face brightened. "Well, in that case, my name is Justin."

He offered his hand, and she shook it.

Ellie and Justin chatted while she sipped her drink, and he guzzled his. The more they talked, the more Ellie wondered if Justin wasn't a bit foxed. He showed no signs of slowing down on his Corona, and she silently prayed he had a designated driver.

Out of nowhere, he blurted out, "Let's dance!"

He grabbed her hand, and she started to protest but then thought about it.

Isn't this why I'm here—to dance and have a little fun?

Justin seemed like a nice enough guy despite being a tad intoxicated. She saw no harm in dancing with him. As the music changed tempo, Justin and Ellie bounced around to the beat, and she laughed.

At the far end of the bar, Pax sat, drinking a ginger ale and watching Ellie. The more he watched her, the more he found himself brooding. He really wished he could have a beer or whiskey—anything to dull the ache of watching her smile, laugh, and flirt with someone other than him. He could never be what she needed. It would be too dangerous to even try. Pax had learned that the hard way a long time ago.

Hell, now, I really need a drink.

The last thing he wanted to think about was his past.

Pax had watched closely as the blond kid approached Ellie. He'd figured she'd be polite and then shoo him away, so he had really been surprised when she continued to chat with him. When they'd gotten up to dance, Pax had almost gone after them, but he'd quickly realized that Ellie had gone willingly.

She seemed to be having fun. He tried to be happy for her, but it was damn hard. He didn't want her to be happy without him. He admitted to himself that it was a selfish thought, but he could live with that. Eventually, he would have to live without Ellie in his life as well. That would be harder to handle, but he'd figure it out.

Just then, a pretty redhead with short curly hair pushed herself up against him, interrupting his thoughts. She pretended to be embarrassed and gave him a flirty apology, offering to make it up to him in several ways.

Pax wasn't in the mood. "No, thanks," he muttered. He signaled the bartender for another drink.

The girl pouted and then said, "Please don't tell me you're gay. Why are all the cute ones gay?"

Pax shook his head at her. "I'm not gay. You just aren't my type." Then, he turned away from her again.

She made an unladylike noise, called him something even more unladylike, and stomped away. A few moments later, Nessa passed by and happened to see him.

"Pax! What are you doing here?" she said as she sat next to him.

Damn!

He wasn't sure he wanted Ellie to know he was here. Nessa expectantly looked at him. Pax glanced up to see where Ellie was, and Nessa followed his line of sight.

"Oh!" said Nessa with a devilish grin.

Pax turned to Nessa. "It's not what it looks like. I just wanted to get out of the house. It's a coincidence that you guys are here, too."

Nessa didn't believe in coincidences. "I'm sure it is," she said with a knowing smile.

She was convinced Pax had it bad for Ellie even if he wouldn't admit it yet. Nessa thought it was time Ellie got a new dance partner.

"Come dance with me, Pax." She grabbed his hand and pulled him away from the bar.

"Nessa, really, this isn't a good idea. I'm a horrible dancer." Pax was not crazy about dancing. More accurately, he hated it.

Nessa pulled him next to her, and he came face-to-face with a guy almost as tall as he was.

Nessa made introductions. "Pax, meet my friend Cain. Cain, meet Ellie's friend Pax."

Cain shifted his eyes a few feet away to where Ellie was dancing with Justin. "Nice to meet you, Pax."

But Cain kept his hands in his pockets, which told Pax he didn't really think it was so nice.

Pax nodded in return. "You, too."

Nessa whispered in Cain's ear. Then, he looked Pax over and walked away.

Pax made a face. "Nessa, what was that about? What are you doing?"

The pace of the music slowed, and Nessa smiled. "I'm dancing with Ellie's friend. Problem?"

Then, she put her arms around Pax. He was noticeably uncomfortable, but he tried to slow dance with her.

The song had only been playing for ten seconds or so when Nessa said, "Can I ask you something?"

Pax nodded.

"Do you love Ellie?"

Pax almost tripped over his own feet. "Um, what? Ellie is a friend, so of course, I care about her."

Nessa rolled her eyes. "That's not what I'm asking. I'm asking if you are in love with her."

Pax was unsure of how to answer.

"I really like you, Pax, and I think you're good for her. But I'm giving you fair warning. Don't ever hurt her. If you do, I'll personally come after you. You do not want to know what kind of skills I have with a cleaver." Nessa gave him a sweet smile. "The only reason Marcus isn't a eunuch is because Ellie begged me to leave him alone."

Pax couldn't help but laugh. "That's too bad. I'd have been happy to hold him down for you." He pretended to think. "In fact, if you're still up for it, my car is outside. We could go find the little jackass right now."

Nessa gave Pax a genuine smile. "Sounds like a great plan."

Ellie's voice interrupted the next sentence before it got started, "Pax?"

Nessa and Pax stopped dancing and turned to see a very confused Ellie standing next to them.

"What are you doing here?" Ellie asked.

Nessa stepped back. "Let's trade partners. I think you two need to talk."

She then pushed Ellie into her spot in front of Pax and grabbed Justin, pulling him away from them to dance elsewhere.

Pax smiled at her. "Would you like to dance?"

Ellie cautiously entered the circle of his arms and placed her hands on his shoulders. Pax instinctively pulled her closer.

Ellie repeated her question. "Why are you here?"

Pax took a moment to answer, savoring the way she felt in his arms. "I wanted a drink, and someone said this was a good place."

He wasn't going to tell her the drink he had been enjoying was something he could have easily gotten from a soda machine.

Ellie didn't look like she believed him, but she didn't comment further. The truth was, she couldn't seem to form words. Pax's hands were on the low of her back, and he was moving his thumbs in small circles. She wasn't even sure he was aware he was doing it.

Ellie needed a distraction. His hands felt too nice.

"So, what were you and Nessa talking about?"

Pax smiled. "Oh, this and that. Nessa is quite a woman."

Ellie nodded. "She's the best. Did I warn you about her?"

Pax looked confused. "Warn me?"

Ellie gave him a conspiratorial look as if she had some big secret. "Well, you know the filter in our brains that tells us when it's inappropriate to say or do something? She doesn't possess one of those. I think she was born without it."

Pax nodded. "I'm learning that about her."

Oh, dear. What did Nessa tell him? Ellie was wondering if she should be worried.

The song ended, and the next one started up. It was another slow song, something Ellie had never heard before.

Pax didn't let her go. "One more dance?"

Ellie looked at him with curiosity. "I thought you hated dancing."

Pax shrugged and pulled her in close. "I thought I did, too. Turns out that it's becoming one of my favorite activities."

Ellie didn't want to enjoy dancing with Pax, but she lost the battle and put her head on his shoulder. Pax smiled and closed his eyes, dedicating every detail to memory—the way she looked, her perfume, the feel of her pressed up against him. He wanted to be able to relive this moment long after her attacker was caught and he had moved on.

Suddenly, Ellie was jerked out of Pax's arms, and Justin stood there, looking angry.

"I think it's time you danced with me again."

He pulled Ellie close and instantly tried to plant a sloppy, wet drunken kiss on her lips. She was pushing him away when he was abruptly pulled in the opposite direction. Pax had him by the shirt collar and was dragging him out the back door. Justin clutched at his collar, trying to breathe. Ellie chased after them.

Pax kicked open the door leading to the alley and tossed Justin to the ground. Then, Pax pulled Justin back up by the front of the shirt and slammed him against the brick wall next to the dumpsters.

His voice was menacing as he warned Justin, "If you ever go near Ellie again, I will personally make sure the next girl you flirt with will be a nurse in the ICU."

Frozen in fear, Justin just stared at Pax.

"Pax!" Ellie yelled as she came stumbling out the back door. "Please don't hurt him. He's drunk. He wasn't thinking. I'm sure he wouldn't have done that if he were sober."

Pax looked back at Ellie and relaxed his grip a tad. "You know him well enough to be sure of that?"

Ellie looked at her hands. "Well, no, but he just doesn't seem like that kind of person."

Pax wasn't convinced. "Maybe he's not a nice guy at all. Maybe I should do the world a favor and kill this scumbag."

Pax pushed his muscular forearm against Justin's throat, and he struggled once again to breathe.

"Please, Pax! Don't!" Ellie's voice rose as she pleaded with him. She gently touched his back. "He didn't hurt me. I'm sure he's learned his lesson. Haven't you, Justin?" Her eyes begged Justin to be smart enough to give the right answer.

Justin nodded the best he could, considering his position against the wall.

Pax dropped Justin, and he fell to the ground in a crumpled heap. Ellie rushed forward to make sure he wasn't dead.

Pax stopped her. "He's fine. Give him a moment to catch his breath."

Ellie watched in concern as Justin managed to sit up, and he began to rub his neck. He shot Pax a dirty look. Then, he promptly leaned toward the dumpster and threw up.

"Serves you right for drinking so much and being a dickweed," Pax muttered. He took Ellie's hand and looked into her eyes. "Are you okay? Really?"

Ellie had a lump in her throat, but she managed to squeak out, "Yes."

Then, she closed her eyes and sighed.

Pax pulled her to him. "Are you ready to go home?"

Ellie sniffled a bit and then nodded. The back door opened once again, and Nessa and Cain exited, the latter looking ready to fight if needed. Pax acknowledged that Cain was likely there to help Ellie, and he decided he liked Cain a little more than before.

Nessa ran to Ellie. "Sweetie! Are you okay? What happened? We turned around, and all three of you were suddenly gone!"

Pax gave a disgusted glare to a sick-looking Justin, still sitting on the ground. "He forgot how to be a gentleman."

Nessa started toward Justin with murder in her eyes. "You sorry, no-good piece of crap!"

Cain grabbed Nessa by the waist and swung her around. "Baby, I think Pax already gave him hell. He looks like he's learned his lesson."

Nessa spit in Justin's general direction and then turned in Cain's arms.

Ellie looked at Nessa. "I'm fine. I promise. I think I'm ready to go home."

Nessa nodded and said, "Let me pay our tab."

Pax spoke up then, "I'll take her home, Nessa. You and Cain stay and enjoy yourselves."

Nessa looked uncertain.

Ellie agreed, "Yes, please don't leave on my account. I'll catch up with you tomorrow."

Cain and Nessa walked back to the door.

"Nessa, hold up. Let me give you money to pay my tab as well," Pax said as he dug out his wallet and his keys. He handed her the bills and then quietly said, "To answer your earlier question, I just might be." Then, he turned to walk Ellie to his Jeep.

Nessa hid a small smile as Cain opened the door for her, and they reentered the bar together.

9

Early the next morning, Ellie knocked on Pax's door. He answered in a pair of sweatpants and looked like he was still partially asleep.

"Hey. Sorry if I woke you," she said softly.

Pax rubbed his hands over his face in an attempt to wake up. "No, you're fine. I overslept. Please come on in." He gestured for her to enter.

Ellie walked in and sat on his love seat.

Pax noticed she seemed nervous. "Everything okay?"

Ellie nodded and gave him a tired smile.

"Would you like some coffee?" he asked. "I was just about to start a pot."

"Yes, that'd be great. Thanks." Ellie fidgeted with the hem of her shirt.

Pax started the coffee and then sat next to her. "So, what did I do to merit such an early morning visit?"

Ellie wanted to tease him about winning the morning visit lotto or some such nonsense, but when she brought her eyes to his, all she could think about was how sexy he looked with tousled hair and his heavily lidded eyes. She needed to concentrate.

"I wanted to thank you again for coming to my rescue last night. You seem to do that a lot." She let out a nervous giggle. "And I was wondering if you have today free. It's my turn to ask for help with something."

Pax grinned at her. "Sure. It's Sunday, and I have absolutely nothing planned. I'm at your service."

"Thank you." She said as she exhaled the breath she didn't realize she'd been holding.

Pax heard the coffee pot stop gurgling. "Sounds like the coffee is done. Be right back." Then he stood up and went into the kitchen to retrieve their drinks. Once he returned, he handed her a cup and taking a sip of his, he asked, "How can I be of assistance?"

"I mostly just need a friend today." She hesitated. "I have to go to my dad's house. The realtor said they have a buyer, so I need to go through the house and make sure all his personal belongings are out." She sighed and looked Pax in the eyes. "I'm just not sure I can do it without some emotional support. I tried to call Nessa, but she's not answering her phone. I'm sure she's still sleeping off last night."

"I'm more than happy to help." Pax drank a little more of his coffee and then yawned. "I'll take a shower and meet you back at your place when I'm ready."

Ellie stood to leave. "Thanks. You don't know how much this means to me."

He smiled at her. "It's my pleasure. Please feel free to stay and finish your coffee. Or you can take it with you, and I'll get the cup later. Either way, it won't take me long to get ready."

She nodded. "I'll just go back to my apartment and finish a few things up before we leave."

"Sounds good. See you in a few." Then Pax disappeared down the hallway, and she heard him turn on the shower. To stop her mind from traveling to places it shouldn't go, Ellie quickly picked up the mug and left Pax's apartment.

Back on her own sofa, she sipped what was left of her coffee and tried not to be nervous. She wondered which brought her more anxiety—spending the day in her dad's house or being alone with Pax. Both seemed to be equally unnerving although for completely different reasons.

Thirty minutes later, Pax and Ellie were en route to Jacob Manchester's house. They pulled into the circle drive, and Pax looked up in admiration at the large Victorian structure. It was an old Queen Anne–style home, complete with octagon towers, turrets, and a rounded large porch. It had been built with a beautiful gray-and-white brick pattern and white stone columns. The grounds were meticulously groomed, and the side garden was full of roses of every type and color. Pax remembered Ellie mentioning that her mom had loved roses. It was such a big home for one person. Pax wondered if Jacob had been lonely, living here by himself.

Ellie pulled a key out of her purse and unlocked the large double doors that opened into the foyer. Pax let out a whistle. There weren't many, if any, houses like this in his little Texas hometown. The delicate crystal chandelier sparkled off the immaculate oak hardwood floors. There was a staircase with intricately carved balusters on both sides of the room, which disappeared into the upper floor. Pax felt a little out of his element.

Ellie sighed and tossed the house keys on the cherry wood console table near the door. She wasn't happy to be here at all, but it was necessary. This visit to this accursed house would be her last, and then it would be out of her life forever. Nothing good had ever happened in this house. There were those fleeting happy moments when she was little, but for the most part, this place was a cesspool of sadness and anger. She could feel it every time she walked through the front doors. Sometimes, it hit her so hard that it took all her strength not to turn and run back out. Today, it felt particularly ominous.

Shaking it off, she turned to Pax and said, "Welcome to Manchester Manor."

Pax had the uneasy feeling that the house was anything but welcoming for Ellie. Her body language was tense, and she had a nervous energy that had only increased once she crossed the threshold. He wanted to ask questions once again, but he stopped himself. She'd offer information if and when she was ready.

Ellie motioned for Pax to follow her. They walked through an archway to the right of the doors, and then she opened a set of double doors that led into a large office area. The room was pretty sparse now that most of Jacob's belongings had been removed. There was only enough furniture left for staging and a few items to give it a personal touch.

Ellie walked to a bookcase and picked up a photo of herself as a little girl playing on the beach. She smiled as she remembered that weekend. It was one of the few good memories she had. A short time before her mother had died, Jacob had surprised them with a weekend away in the Florida Keys. Ellie had always loved the ocean, so she'd spent most of her weekend playing in the water and hoping to find shells and tide pools. She'd especially loved it when she found a horseshoe crab. She had been careful to only watch it, never touching it.

A flood of emotions came rushing back, and Ellie felt tears starting to fall. Pax walked up behind her and realized she was crying. He turned her around and pulled her into a hug. She was embarrassed and stepped away.

"Ellie, this is why I'm here, correct? To be your emotional support? Let me be here for you. You can lean on me, and I promise never to let you down."

She nodded as she wiped away a fresh tear. She gave him a wobbly smile and sat on the padded window seat that faced the side gardens. She ran her fingers over the fabric of the cushion.

"This used to be my favorite spot. Dad would sit at the desk and work. I'd ask him if I could work, too." Ellie sniffled a bit and then continued, "He'd say, 'Ellie girl, you only get one childhood, so enjoy it for as long as you can. You'll have plenty of time to work when you're grown.' Then, he'd kiss the tip of my nose and tell me to enjoy a book by the window until he was free to play with me." She swiped at her eyes once more. "He'd sit over here by me, and most of the time, he'd pretend I beat him at checkers. I knew he'd let me win, but I didn't care. It was time with my daddy, and that was all that mattered."

Pax walked to the window seat and sat beside her. "It sounds like he was a great father."

Ellie nodded. "He was...until Mom died. Then, everything changed." She steeled herself.

Maybe it would help if she talked about that day. She could confide in Pax. She knew that. Whatever else might or might not be between them, she never doubted that he was a true friend.

She inhaled a deep breath. "My mother was killed upstairs. I was seven, and I was supposed to be in the playroom that evening. But like all kids, I loved to pretend. That night, I took some of my toys into the upstairs library and pretended I was looking for secret passages. I recall moving a couple of books around and telling my doll that we found the entrance. We had this large antique sofa in there, and it was just high enough off the floor that I could get underneath. So, I grabbed my doll and a flashlight and scooted under until I was completely hidden. Shortly afterward, I heard the door open and close, and I listened to my mom arguing with a man. He was very angry, and it scared me. He kept calling her horrible names. He said she was a liar and a slut."

Ellie's heart raced a bit as she remembered the scene. She took a moment to get her emotions back under control. Pax waited patiently for her to continue. The look of concern in his eyes gave her the courage to keep going.

"I saw their shoes. They were standing close to each other. Then, I heard him slap my mom and tell her she needed to confess the truth. Mom cried a little, but she said she'd already told everyone who needed to know. Suddenly, he threw her to the floor and was on top of her, choking her. I just froze, Pax. I couldn't help her. I couldn't scream. While hiding under that sofa, I watched him strangle the life out of her."

Ellie broke then. She began to sob, and Pax reached out to hold her.

"I didn't help her, Pax! I didn't do anything! I was a coward!"

"Ellie, you were seven years old, for God's sake. You can't possibly believe you could have done anything to stop it. He probably would have killed you, too, if he'd known you were there." Pax let her go and handed her a box of tissues sitting on a nearby shelf.

Ellie dabbed at her eyes. "I know you're right. My therapist told me the same thing. I just can't help but think I should have tried."

Pax pushed a strand of hair back from her face. "I take it, you didn't recognize the man."

It was more of a statement than a question.

Ellie shook her head and blew her nose. "No. I'll admit, something was familiar about his voice, but I didn't get a good look at him from my hiding spot. I wouldn't be able to identify him at all."

She clasped her hands on her lap and studied her fingers. "I think he suspected I was in the room somewhere. He found my other toys still sitting on top of the sofa. I thought he was gonna look underneath the sofa, and I was terrified he would find me. Then, I heard my father's voice coming from down the hall. The man heard Daddy, too, and quickly left through the door on the other side of the room. I was still too scared to leave my hiding spot, so I just curled up with my doll and cried over my mother. My dad came into the room minutes later and found Mom. That was when I had the courage to crawl out."

Pax knew that had been hard for Ellie to share, and he felt honored that she trusted him with these memories, horrific as they were. Ellie stood up then and spent a few moments picking up little items that had belonged to her dad.

She placed them on the desk. "I guess we'll need to grab a few boxes from the basement when we're ready to pack this stuff up. I think a few are still down there."

Pax nodded.

With a smile, she tried to put on a cheerier expression. She did feel lighter after talking to Pax, so that was somewhat relieving.

She took his hand and led him out of the office and to the stairs. "I have something cool to show you. Come with me."

Pax gladly followed, enjoying the feel of Ellie's hand in his. They went up the stairs, and she led him to a door at the left end of the hallway. After pushing the door open in a dramatic fashion, she pulled him inside. It was a large room with windows lining up one entire wall. Brilliant sunshine lit up the room.

"This was my playroom." She let go of his hand and walked toward the middle of the room. She made a slow circle and enjoyed the warmth of the sun on her face. "I loved this room so much. I fought pirates, found treasure, and slayed dragons in here." She smiled wide. "My dad and I even had this scavenger hunt game." She walked toward one of the windows at the end of the room and knelt down. "There's a panel right here in the wall, and if you hit it just right..." Ellie bumped it with the side of her fist, and it popped open. "He used to hide clues in here for me."

Pax walked up behind her and peered down as she fully opened the hidden door. He squinted his eyes, trying to see into the darkness. "Ellie, I think something is in there." Kneeling down beside her, he reached inside and pulled out a box covered in dust.

Ellie's eyes went wide. *When had Dad put that in there?*

After her mom had died, her dad had stopped playing with her. All he had done was drink and grieve. When she'd lost her mother, she'd also lost her father. As Ellie had grown up, she'd realized that it wasn't totally his fault. Drinking had been his way of coping with the grief just as her method had been to often pretend her mom was still with them. She'd focus on a spot in the room, pretend her mom was there, and then carry on a conversation. She'd tell the imaginary Mary Manchester all about her day at school or what boy had talked to her or how she was looking forward to the latest dance. Her therapist, Dr. Andrews, had assured her that it was okay to continue these pretend conversations as long as they allowed her to vent her feelings, and she understood that they weren't real.

As her preteen years had faded away, Ellie had felt it was time to put away her imaginary mom—not because she didn't miss her mom anymore, but because she needed to move on. She'd spent many years crying and mourning the things that would never be. She had grown into a big girl, and it had been time to behave like one. At least, that had been the facade she'd put on for the rest of the world. Inside, she had still felt like the frightened, lonely little girl who needed her parents.

Ellie was afraid to open the box. She had no clue what could be inside, and she wasn't sure she wanted to know. It was dusty, but it didn't actually look like it had been there for long. The box appeared to be fairly new. She looked up at Pax, and their eyes met. The emotional turmoil must have been evident on her face because he tried to reassure her.

"It's like one last gift from your father. Would you prefer I open it?"

Ellie swallowed and nodded. "Please."

Pax loosened the lid and slid it off to one side. Inside, he found files, photos, and letters. It all appeared to be information pertaining to her mother's murder case. Pax handed the folder to Ellie, and then he took another folder and started scanning through it.

Ellie looked confused. "Why would Dad leave me all this? The case had gone cold, and after several years, I'd thought he'd given up."

Pax looked at other items in the box. "Looks like he worked on it right up until his accident." He held up a sheet of paper. "This letter says he recently had some handwriting analyzed and to call this number when he was ready to discuss the results." He rifled through the rest of the paperwork, looking for more information on the handwriting. He knew this might lead him to Ellie's assailant as well. Disappointed, he tossed the rest of the documents back into the box. "Nothing else about that in here."

Ellie was still trying to process it all. "Pax, what if my dad figured it out? What if he knew who killed my mother?"

Pax glanced down at the box. "I guess it's possible."

Ellie reached for Pax and grasped his arm. She looked pale.

"Ted told me he thought my father's crash wasn't an accident. What if…what if Ted was right? What if Daddy figured it out and someone killed him?"

Pax covered her hand with his. "If that's the case, then we need to be careful about who we trust with this information."

Ellie looked at Pax through unshed fresh tears.

Pax gave her hand a reassuring squeeze. "Don't worry, Ellie. We'll figure this out. I'll do whatever it takes to help you."

She leaned forward and hugged him. "Thank you, Pax. Thank you so much." Then, she pulled back and impulsively placed a kiss on his lips.

Pax froze. He wanted to kiss her back. In fact, he wanted to do a lot more than that, but this wasn't the time. She was vulnerable, and it wouldn't be safe for either of them to let their emotions cloud their judgment. He gave her a hug and quickly released her.

Ellie was embarrassed. "Sorry. I shouldn't have done that."

Pax smiled at her and tried to lessen the awkwardness. "It's fine. I was just afraid to kiss you back. You might get addicted to me, and we can't have that. You know what they say…"

Ellie's face registered annoyance at his arrogance.

Perfect. That's safer than gratitude, thought Pax.

"Once you go Pax, you never go back," he finished.

She dramatically rolled her eyes and smacked him with the box lid. "I'm pretty sure no one says that. You really are insufferable sometimes, you know it?"

Pax just smiled.

"Yeah, you know it," replied Ellie. "Well, I guess we should get this stuff down to the car and then work on the other rooms."

"Sounds good," said Pax. "We'll deal with our discovery once you've put this house behind you."

Ellie agreed. She didn't have the energy for more than one emotional upheaval at a time.

10

Ellie and Pax carried a few things to the car and put them in the trunk. Walking back inside, Ellie mentioned the need for more boxes, so Pax offered to get them from the basement while she went back upstairs to go through her dad's bedroom. It'd turned out there was a lot more of her dad's belongings than she'd realized, but they had made quick work of most of it in a short amount of time.

Pax flipped on the light in the staircase leading to the lowest floor. As he took that first step, something solid hit him hard on the back of the head. He tumbled down the long stairway, head over heels, and hit the door at the bottom. The impact knocked the door open, and his unconscious body rolled inside. Footsteps followed him down, and then a man's booted foot kicked Pax to be sure he was out.

Upstairs, Ellie was unaware of the commotion happening below. She was digging through a drawer in her father's nightstand.

"Dad, why did you keep all this junk?" Ellie muttered to herself. She pulled the drawer out and dumped its entire contents into a box, determined to sift through it later.

The closet was her next target, so she began looking through the few boxes still inside. It appeared her dad had kept several boxes of her old art projects. She smiled to herself. He'd always bragged on her paintings, macaroni creations, and primitive clay sculptures, but she'd never expected him to still have them after all these years. Pulling a couple of more boxes off a shelf, she set them on the floor and gave them a quick inspection.

Ellie heard the floorboards creaking behind her, and she assumed Pax had entered the room.

Still working toward the back of the closet, she called out, "Pax, you won't believe the stuff I found in here. Dad kept all my old masterpieces." When he didn't reply, she yelled a little louder, "Pax? Did you hear me?"

It was still silent, but she was sure she'd heard someone enter the bedroom. Getting up from the floor, she dusted her hands off on her jeans and walked out of the closet. No one was in the room, so she shrugged it off, thinking she'd imagined it. She turned back toward the closet, but before she could take a step, she was roughly pushed inside, and the door was slammed behind her.

Ellie hit the floor and knocked over a couple of the smaller boxes. "What the hell?" She got up and attempted to open the door, but it wouldn't move.

She tried to remain calm. *Who would have locked me in the closet? And why? And where was Pax?* She knew he wouldn't have played this kind of prank on her, not after knowing all she'd been through in this house. He was ornery, but he wasn't cruel. It couldn't have been him.

Ellie banged on the door and screamed, "Hey! Let me out! This isn't funny! Let me out now!"

All was quiet on the other side of the door.

"Pax! Pax, can you hear me?" Her voice was panicked.

Utilizing the breathing techniques Dr. Andrews had taught her, Ellie tried to envision her safe place.

Within a few minutes, she had managed to calm her heart rate and breathing down enough to avoid a panic attack or hyperventilation.

Ellie patted her pockets, looking for her cell phone, but she quickly realized it was out in the car, so she couldn't call for help. Using her shoulder, she tried ramming the door, but it wouldn't budge. All she was doing was giving herself bruises. She sat down with her back against the door, wrapped her arms around her knees, and waited.

Pax's eyes fluttered open, and he tried to focus, which turned out to be difficult. He wasn't sure what he was looking at. He thought maybe it was a ceiling.

Why do I feel like I've just been run through a spin cycle?

He slowly raised his hand to his head, feeling for injuries. Wincing, he found a large knot. Pulling his hand away, he also discovered some blood although it was obvious he wasn't bleeding profusely.

Pax managed to get himself into a sitting position, and he looked around. He was in the basement.

How did I—

Someone hit me! Oh no! I need to find Ellie!

Pax got to his feet. He was slightly unsteady, and his vision was still a little fuzzy, but he made his way up the stairs. Entering the foyer, he went straight to Jacob's old office. What few items were left in the room had been smashed or thrown to the floor.

Pax called for Ellie but heard nothing. With a lump in his throat, he ran back into the foyer and then stopped in his tracks. He smelled smoke. Something was on fire.

Overcome by adrenaline, he took the stairs two at a time until he reached the second floor. Smoke was billowing out of the playroom. He pulled his cell phone from his pocket and called 911. He gave them all the info they needed and quickly hung up.

He had to find Ellie. He went as far as he could toward the playroom before the flames pushed him back. He was doing his best to tamp down his fear. He silently prayed that she wasn't in there. *Please, God, just let her be okay. Let me find her.*

"Ellie! Ellie, where are you?"

He shouted her name as he opened each door, making his way down the hall. Every room had been ransacked and was filling with smoke. For a moment, he thought he heard a faint pounding sound. When he reached Jacob's old bedroom, he saw that it was smoked filled as well. He heard the pounding once again and knew it had to be her. He coughed as he fought his way through the clouds of acrid air burning his lungs.

Then, he noticed a chair lodged under the doorknob of the closet. Pulling it away and opening the door, he found Ellie inside. She looked up at him from her position on the floor, the relief on her face obvious.

Pax quickly pulled her to her feet. "Thank God! We have to get out of here now, Ellie."

She appeared to be in shock, so he lifted her in his arms and carried her out of the room. Getting her safely downstairs and out of the house, Pax set her on the hood of the car.

"Are you okay?" He looked her over for signs of smoke inhalation or injury.

She nodded but still seemed to be in shock. Her hands were bruised, and her eyes were puffy and red from crying.

He could hear the sirens approaching from a few blocks away. Ellie seemed to snap out of it then. She grabbed Pax and pulled him to her. Then, she wrapped her arms and legs around him. She buried her face in his shoulder and held on tight. He hugged her back and kissed the top of her head.

"It's gonna be okay, Ellie. I promise. We'll figure out what's going on." He realized the fire trucks would need room. "We need to move the car, okay?"

She nodded and reluctantly let go of her grip on Pax. He put his hands on her waist and helped her to the ground. Then, he opened the passenger door for her. Once she was safely inside, he ran to the driver's side, fired up the engine, and moved the car out of the driveway, parking it farther down the street.

He turned to Ellie. "I need to go back to the house."

Ellie gripped his hand. "No! Don't leave me! I'll go with you."

He raised his free hand to her face and cupped her chin. Looking into her eyes, he said, "I swear to always be here when you need me, Ellie. Always."

Pax knew this was a promise he shouldn't have made, but he couldn't have stopped himself. No matter what separated them, if she needed him, he'd find a way to come back to her.

She gave him a small smile, and he moved his hands to either side of her face, pulling her forward. Ellie thought he was going to kiss her, but instead of claiming her lips, he pressed his lips to her forehead in a chaste kiss. She was surprised at how much that had disappointed her.

"Let's go find out what the hell happened, shall we?" said Pax as he opened his door.

Mustering her strength, she opened her own door and climbed out. Pax locked up, and they walked back toward the house. As they got closer and could see the flames, Ellie's steps faltered. For courage, she took Pax's hand.

He tried not to read anything into her sudden need for physical contact. He knew it was likely because she needed reassurance and not because she wanted to touch him, but he so badly wanted it to be the latter. It frustrated him that even in such a horrible situation, he still couldn't keep himself from wanting her. There were a hundred other things he should be thinking about, but instead, his mind was cycling through mental pictures of them together. It happened every time they touched and pretty much any other time he thought of or looked at her.

They rounded the corner of the open gates to see the firemen already hard at work. Flames were shooting out of the roof and windows on the top floor. Despite the torrent of water drowning the house, the fire continued to leap and arch in various directions.

To Ellie, it seemed futile. She continued to tightly grip Pax's hand, so he pulled her close, let go of her hand, and hugged her.

"I'm sorry about the house, Ellie."

She gazed up at him and started softly laughing. Pax wasn't sure he'd heard her correctly.

Is she actually laughing?

"Ellie? Are you sure you're okay?"

Ellie stepped back from his embrace, wrapping her arms around herself, and looked at the house. "Pax, I've always hated this house. It held so many sad memories. While I wouldn't have wished for it to burn down, I'm not gonna miss it. This actually seems like a fitting end to a horrible legacy. It's almost poetic."

Weighing her words, Pax saw her point. "Yeah, I guess so."

He put his arm around her again as a police officer approached them. It was time to give another statement.

Pax was beyond angry. He was going to kill whoever was behind all this. The attacks had to stop, and he was going to make sure they did.

The fire was eventually doused to nothing but smoke and wet ashes. Fire Chief Mark Reynolds told Ellie that his department would have to wait until it was safe to enter and do an inspection, but he suspected the house was a loss. Ellie had figured as much. Oddly enough, she was fine with that.

Talking to Pax that morning, she felt like she'd finally let go of so much. Shaking free of it in that house and then watching it burn was like all her cares and worries had burned up with it. There was that pesky matter of who had tried to burn them to death, but at the moment, even that seemed trivial. She felt lighter and more optimistic than she had in years. She had Pax to thank for that—and for a lot of things lately.

Pax had moved to a garden bench several feet away, and he was talking on the phone. She watched him as he animatedly conversed with whoever was on the other end. He was upset, and she assumed his conversation had to do with the fire. He ran his hands through his hair, mussing it and causing several clumps to stick up. She thought he looked adorable when he did that. He ended the call, leaned his head back, and closed his eyes in frustration.

Ellie moved to sit beside him. "Everything okay?"

Pax opened his eyes and sighed. "Yeah, I'm just searching for answers."

Ellie nodded. "Who was that?"

Pax cleared his throat. "A friend. I thought he could help."

He didn't elaborate further, and Ellie suspected he wasn't going to.

Changing the subject, Pax asked, "Are you ready to go home? Are you hungry?"

Ellie realized she was starving. "Yes, I'm famished. We should eat."

They walked back to the car in silence. Pax opened the door for Ellie, and she sat down and buckled up. As he walked to the driver's side, he stopped for a moment and took a deep breath.

His call with Ted hadn't gone well. Ted had been angry with Pax and had accused him of dropping the ball. Pax was angry at himself, too. He knew he had been letting his feelings get in the way, and it had kept him from thinking straight. He shouldn't have let Ellie go anywhere alone, even in that big house.

She wouldn't be safe anywhere until he caught the bastard behind all this. To top things off, he still couldn't tell Ellie the truth. If Ted didn't give the okay soon, Pax was going to do it anyway.

Screw the job. He'd protect her regardless of what Ted did or didn't do, but he couldn't continue to lie to her.

Pax lowered himself into the driver's seat and buckled up, then reached over to give Ellie's hand a reassuring squeeze. "How does Chinese sound?"

She returned the squeeze. "Sounds great."

Pax pulled onto the roadway and drove toward the only Chinese restaurant in town.

After picking up their take-out, they went back to her apartment to eat and sort through the few boxes they'd managed to save before the fire. They'd only gotten through one box when Ellie pulled out the smaller box her father had hidden in the wall. Pax cleared the coffee table, so they could spread everything out in front of them, and then he sat beside her on the sofa. Ellie pored over the information, looking for anything that seemed familiar.

"I don't know, Pax. I was so little when this happened. I don't know that I remember enough about the people in our lives for any of this to make sense to me. You think this person was someone my father knew?"

Pax expelled a frustrated breath. It had to be someone Jacob had known. This person knew a secret—something worth attempted blackmail, something that might have been worth murdering Mary Manchester. Someone Jacob had suspected would match the handwriting in the letters he'd received.

"It's okay, Ellie. We'll keep looking. There's bound to be a hint here somewhere."

They spent the next couple of hours reading police reports and Jacob's notes and talking about possible motives until they were both tired and feeling somewhat defeated. Pax suggested they take a break, and Ellie was more than happy to comply.

Pax went into her kitchen and found a bottle of wine and two glasses. He poured some for them both, and then he sat down and tried to mentally piece together all the information they'd gathered with what he'd already gotten from Ted.

Pax struggled to form a complete picture, but it wouldn't take shape. Something was still missing. He needed to call the number they'd found and see the results from the handwriting analysis.

Pax looked up to find Ellie staring at him. He gave her his usual lazy smile, and she smiled back. There was something different in her smile, something he hadn't sensed before.

She broke eye contact and drank what was left of her wine. She turned toward him again and said, "We need to talk."

11

Pax silently worried she was going to push him away again. Or maybe she needed to clarify boundaries. She had been through a lot today, and she had leaned on him for emotional and physical support. He probably should have been the first to bring it up, but he hadn't wanted to spoil the comfortable and intimate companionship they currently had going. It had been nice having someone confide in him the way Ellie had today.

Ellie reached for Pax's hands and scooted closer to him. She looked into his eyes and gave him a nervous smile. He was slightly relieved, thinking that smile was a good sign. She interlaced her fingers with his and then leaned in close.

"Pax, I owe you so much. You've been a good friend. You've been the protector I didn't even know I needed. And you've helped me learn how to move on from my past."

Pax shifted uncomfortably. The truth of his purpose in her life was hanging over him like a heavy anvil, waiting to drop at any moment. "Ellie, I don't need or deserve your thanks. I just—"

Ellie interrupted him by letting go of one of his hands and placing a well-manicured finger on his lips. "Just hush, and let me finish."

Pax nodded.

She pulled her finger away and grasped his hand once more. "Trapped in that closet, all I could think about was how I might die and how you might already be dead. I thought about missed opportunities. I thought about how I haven't really been living life." Ellie chuckled. "Nessa is constantly badgering me to get out and have some fun or meet someone. But fear has always kept me from trying. I didn't want to meet anyone after Marcus. And when my dad died, the wall I'd built around my heart grew even taller. I wanted to stay in my safe, protected fortress. But I can't do that, Pax. It's not living. Life means taking risks and experiencing every opportunity to the fullest. You've helped me see that."

Pax smiled at her. "Glad I could help."

Ellie raised a hand to his cheek, her expression serious. "Pax, you seem to have done what my therapist couldn't. Don't you see? I finally feel like this oppressive burden is lighter. I can't say it's completely gone, but for the first time in years, I feel..." She struggled for the right words. "I feel less afraid. I feel like I have a chance at being truly happy again. Fear has ruled my life for far too long."

Pax let her words sink in. *Is she saying I make her happy?* He was glad yet not glad. He wasn't a permanent fixture in anyone's life. He couldn't be what she needed. He would always be her friend, if she would still allow it once this mess was over, but he could never be more. His past had taught him that. He removed her hand from his cheek, then held it, looking at her fingers instead of meeting her eyes.

"Ellie, listen. I'm not…I mean…I can't…" He didn't know what to say.

She shook her head and laughed. "Pax, calm down. I'm not proposing marriage or even a relationship. I'm just saying that I'm ready to take steps, move forward, and live it up a little."

Pax raised his head, but still looked confused.

Ellie framed his face with her hands. "I don't want regrets. I don't want to someday look back and wish I'd done something. I don't want to wish I'd done this." Then, she leaned into him and kissed him.

Pax's arms wrapped around her of their own accord even though his brain screamed no. He deepened the kiss and tasted her. Since the day he'd pushed her against the bedroom door, all he'd wanted to do was kiss her again. She was his drug, and he desperately wanted another fix.

She maneuvered herself until she was straddling his lap, and then she continued to kiss him. He broke the kiss and pulled away. His face revealed his conflicted emotions—a mixture of agony and ecstasy. He knew this couldn't go any further, but he needed a little more of her. He just wanted to touch her for a while longer. He told himself he'd stop before it went too far.

Ellie was thrilled to see her desire reflected back in Pax's brilliant blue eyes. He wanted her as bad as she wanted him. She crossed her arms as she reached down and grabbed the hem of her shirt. Then, she pulled it over her head and tossed it behind her. Pax's mouth went dry at the sight before him.

Ellie leaned into him and whispered in his ear, "Maybe you should take me to the bedroom."

When he didn't move, she tried again. "I want you, Pax," she said his name like a caress before nipping at his earlobe.

Pax felt his restraint starting to snap. Grasping her upper arms, he held her away from him and looked into her lovely brown eyes. "Ellie, we can't do this. We've already talked about it. This isn't a step we should take." His head meant the words, but the rest of his body certainly didn't agree. He was aroused and wanted her more than he'd ever wanted anyone in his life.

Ellie's face fell a little. "I don't care about those reasons anymore. They don't matter. I'm not sure they ever did. I want to live, Pax. Please…help me feel alive again."

Her last sentence sounded like a plea. Knowing she was all but begging for him, his last semblance of control disappeared.

Pax stood up, taking her with him. She wrapped her legs around his waist, and he walked toward the bedroom, stopping in the hall to push her against the wall. He ground his body into hers as he kissed down her neck and shoulders.

Unlike last time, she was ready for more. She buried her hands in his hair and guided him lower. Pax slid one bra strap down her arm and then the other one, allowing him full access to her mostly naked torso. She moaned as he kissed and licked a trail from one side to the other. He returned to her lips and kissed her until they were both breathless.

Then, he pulled back and leaned his forehead against hers. "Damn, Ellie. You're gonna be the death of me. I know I shouldn't, but I can't stop myself. I've wanted you for too long. You're all I can think about. You've consumed my soul. Every fiber of my being belongs to you."

Ellie gave him a wicked smile as she unbuttoned his shirt. His breath hitched as she explored the contours of his bare chest with her fingers.

"I've thought about you, too, Pax. I've dreamed about you, about us."

Pax lifted her away from the wall and carried her into the bedroom. "Maybe you should show me what we did in your dreams. Then, I'll show you what we did in mine."

The next morning, Ellie awoke to the beautiful bright sun shining through her bedroom windows. Her room somehow seemed different this morning. Maybe she had never really paid attention to how it looked in the mornings. Maybe it was because she'd gotten her first great night of sleep in ages.

She stretched her slightly sore limbs. Or maybe it was because she'd had a full night of passion with Tanner Paxton. She was pretty sure Pax had caused her new outlook. Last night had been amazing. Even when she'd thought she was in love with Marcus, sex had never been that good.

Smiling, she mentally slapped herself for waiting so long. She should have let Pax finish what he'd started the day when she was almost kidnapped. Oddly enough, even that memory couldn't dampen her mood this morning. Life felt more than bearable for a change.

A naked Pax walked out of the bathroom and saw that she was awake. He crawled back into bed and pulled her into his arms, enjoying the feel of her body against his. "Good morning, beautiful."

She smiled. He was so sweet to her.

"Good morning, tall, dark, and sexy," she replied as she ran her hand up his chest and around his neck.

Pax laughed and then thoroughly kissed her.

When he pulled away, she was sure they were going to end up in bed for a few hours more, but Pax surprised her by saying, "Get that sweet body dressed. We have a busy day ahead of us."

Then, he got out of bed and started putting on his clothes.

Ellie wasn't sure she wanted to leave the bedroom yet, so she sat up and let the sheet fall down. It pooled at her waist, leaving her upper body bare.

Attempting what she hoped was a sultry pout, she said, "Do we have to go right now? Couldn't we stay in bed a little longer?"

Pax turned to answer her and froze in place. Her display had just the effect she had been hoping for.

He walked toward her but stopped short of actually reaching her. "I'd love nothing more than to spend all day keeping you occupied in that bed, but we have things to do."

Ellie was disappointed. "We do? I don't remember making plans."

Pax gave her a sly grin. "Actually, I made them. I thought you could use a day away from it all. Is that okay?"

She had to admit that sounded like a great idea. Pax walked over, pulled her into his arms, and gave her a surprisingly gentle kiss. She looked into his face and swore she saw something more than lust lurking in the depths of his eyes.

He whispered across her lips, "You're so beautiful."

She felt beautiful. He made her feel cherished. She hadn't felt that way in so long. She knew it really meant nothing, but every time he said or did something thoughtful, warmth would spread through her like a blanket of happiness. It was probably silly, but she decided that from here on out, she would embrace the silly as much as the sensible.

She playfully pushed him away. "Flattery will get you everywhere. As for these plans, do I have time for a shower?" she asked as she untangled her legs from the bedsheets.

He looked at his watch. "I think we can allow that. I need to get some clean clothes from my apartment anyway. I'll be back in a few minutes."

Ellie stood up and yawned. "Great." She walked into the bathroom and turned on the shower.

Pax grabbed her key and left the apartment, locking up behind him. He unlocked and entered his own apartment just as his cell phone rang.

"Hello?" Pax said as he tossed both sets of keys on the counter. He entered his bedroom.

"Pax, it's Ted. How is Ellie this morning? Have you talked to her?"

Pax smiled to himself, thinking about the night before. He'd had sex plenty of times, but last night had been unlike anything he'd ever experienced. It had been incredible. Ellie was incredible.

"Yeah, she's okay. I'm spending the day with her. I think I've got a lead on our blackmailer, and I'm gonna follow up on that today."

Ted's voice piqued with interest. "A good lead? Finally! What have you learned?"

Pax hesitated. "Well, I'm not sure until I check it out. I promise to tell you more once I have something solid."

Ted wasn't happy that Pax was withholding any kind of information, but Pax was just doing his job, so Ted couldn't really fault him for that.

"Okay, Pax. Just let me know as soon as you learn something helpful. And take good care of my girl. No more close calls, ya got it?"

"Got it."

Pax hung up the phone and made a couple more quick calls to set the day in motion. Then, he decided a shower would do him some good as well. He'd really rather grab his clothes, cross the hall, and get in the shower with Ellie, but he knew that would only lead to them staying home, and he needed to check on that lead as soon as possible.

He'd called Mattie earlier that morning, while Ellie was still sleeping, and made arrangements for a picnic lunch. She had happily packed it full of Ellie's favorite foods, then had it delivered to Pax's apartment. A short time later, Pax had placed the loaded cooler in the backseat of the Jeep.

Ellie climbed in, put on her sunglasses, and gave Pax a dazzling smile. He cranked the engine and pulled out of his parking spot.

"So, where are we going? It's been ages since I've really gone anywhere, even for a day."

Pax could sense her excitement, and it was infectious. He loved seeing her so happy and vibrant. It really did seem that she'd let go of all the burdens holding her back. Pax found himself a little envious. He wished he could do the same, but he wasn't sure it was possible for him. He feared he was too damaged.

During the hour and a half drive, they talked about places they had both visited. Pax talked about his trips to Arizona and the time his parents had taken him to New York City. Ellie talked about her family's visits to the Florida coast. She told him all about her love of the ocean and that when she was little, she'd wanted to be a marine biologist. Pax could easily envision a lovely little girl with big dark brown eyes, exploring the tide pools for signs of life.

"What stopped you from chasing your dream?" asked Pax.

They pulled off the main road and headed toward a camping area at Eufaula Lake. Ellie looked at their surroundings, and Pax could tell she was thrilled with his location choice.

Turning back to him, she said, "I guess after my mom died, I didn't want to be near the ocean anymore. It reminded me of her too much."

Taking in the large lake materializing before them, she changed the subject. "So, have you always wanted to work in security?"

Pax found the spot he had been looking for and put the Jeep in park. Turning off the ignition, he stared at the keys in his hand for a moment. Raising his eyes to hers, he finally answered, "No. Security sorta chose me."

Ellie had the feeling he wasn't comfortable talking about this topic. Although she wanted to know more about this part of his life, she wouldn't push.

Pax spoke up again before the silence became awkward, "What I really wanted to be was a male stripper."

Ellie's mouth fell open, and then she realized he was teasing her. She rolled her eyes. "Jerk," she muttered as she opened her door.

Pax laughed and grabbed the food. "Let's eat. This jerk is hungry."

Spreading a blanket out on a soft patch of grass, Pax set the cooler down and pulled out all the mouthwatering food Mattie had prepared. He piled Ellie's plate with fried chicken, coleslaw, and baked beans, and then he filled his own plate. He handed her a water bottle and settled in to enjoy the meal and the company.

They made short work of the lunch before them. This particular spot was fairly remote, so they had it all to themselves. Pax would love to take advantage of their seclusion, but he knew his contact could arrive at any moment. As if on cue, an elderly man walked out of the cluster of trees behind them with a fishing pole in one hand and a tackle box in the other.

Ellie looked up and smiled as the man approached them.

Pax gave him a friendly nod. "Is the fishing good here?"

The man shrugged. "Sometimes, it is. I don't get out here often. But I have a feeling that today will be my lucky day."

Pax tried to hide his excitement. *Lucky day* was the term they had agreed upon, which meant he had the information Pax was looking for.

Ellie looked at Pax. "You should have brought a pole and some tackle."

He nodded in agreement. "Too bad I didn't." He stared up at the man standing over them. "What are they biting on right now?"

Pushing his tan bucket hat back, off his forehead, the stranger scratched the day-old stubble on his chin. "I've been doing well with minnows, but I have some lures that have landed a whopper or two in the last couple of weeks. I'd be glad to show you my gear, if you want to take a look."

Pax glanced at Ellie. "Would you mind? I promise to be right back."

She gave Pax a brilliant smile. "Go on. I'm enjoying just soaking up this sunshine."

Pax leaned down for a quick kiss, and then he walked to the edge of the water with the man he knew as Greg. They were far enough away that Ellie wouldn't hear their conversation.

Greg set his tackle box on a stump removed the top tray. He pulled out some lures and pretended to show them to Pax while filling him in on the details he'd learned.

"It took some money, but I got the guy at the analysis place to give me the handwriting samples and results. I don't know how much it will help. The samples are numbered, so no names are attached to them. But maybe you can find the matching identities somewhere."

Pax nodded and accepted the envelope from Greg's hand. Pax folded it up, glanced toward Ellie to make sure she wasn't watching, and then stuffed it into his back pocket. "Thanks, Greg. I owe you one."

Greg scrutinized Pax for a moment. "Pax, we go way back, and you know I'd never tell you how to protect a client, but this seems different. You're emotionally invested."

Pax started to protest, but Greg held up his hand. "I didn't say that was a bad thing. I'm just telling you to be careful. Why is this girl being kept in the dark?"

Pax let out a discouraged sigh. "The man who hired me insists that she wouldn't let me protect her if she knew the truth."

Greg shook his head in concern. "Boy, that is a recipe for disaster, and you know it, especially if she means anything to you at all." He paused and carefully weighed his next sentence. "Carrie would want you to be happy."

Pax winced. "I know, Greg. I know. I just have to figure out how to fix it."

Greg cast a lure into the water to keep up the pretense. "So, why are we meeting out here? I could have come to your apartment."

Pax frowned. "I'm not really sure who I can trust right now. I need to take extra precautions until I figure it out."

Greg nodded in understanding. "Take care, Pax. Let me know if you need me for anything else."

Pax stared into the water for a moment. Then, he turned and walked back to Ellie. He looked at her beautiful form as she reclined on the blanket, her face tilted toward the sun. Guilt squeezed his heart like a vise. He needed to get the facts together, so he could tell her the truth. So far, those facts had been difficult to acquire, but he might finally have a piece that would tie some things together. He could only hope she'd understand.

12

The sun had started to set over the lake when Ellie and Pax decided it was time to head home. There was a chill in the air, and Pax gave Ellie his jacket. She wrapped it around herself and comfortably settled into her seat. Before they even made it twenty miles, she was asleep next to him.

Pax occasionally glanced at her, and his heart swelled. He wasn't sure what to do with these feelings that he knew he shouldn't have for her. Despite his best efforts, he worried that he was falling in love with Ellie. Normal people would be happy about that, but he wasn't normal.

He used to be just another kid in juvenile detention. He'd run with a bad group of kids and happened to be in the wrong place at the wrong time. He hadn't participated in the theft. Hell, he hadn't even realized what was happening until it was about over. By that time, the cops had been everywhere, and he had been implicated as an accomplice.

Thinking back, that was actually what had turned his life around. Pax was one hell of a fighter. It was part of why he had been so popular with the group. Regardless of who had started a fight with them, Pax had always finished it. His battle scars were like badges of honor.

Then, Greg had noticed his talents and mentored him. Once he had been released from juvie, Greg had taught him to channel all that anger and strength into something positive—protecting the innocent. But this job had come with its own set of scars, and it wasn't always Pax who paid that price.

Pax looked at Ellie once again. If anyone ever needed protecting, it was Ellie. Something serious was going down, and she didn't realize that the perpetrator might be right under her nose. As soon as he knew what was happening, he was going to tell her everything. She'd probably be pissed, and she would have every right to be, but he didn't think he could continue to do as Ted had asked. Pax couldn't carry this out to the end and eventually walk away without her ever knowing the truth. She deserved better.

It was dark when Pax pulled the Jeep into his parking spot at Rose Hill.

Ellie yawned and stretched. "Wow. I didn't realize I was so tired." She looked at her watch and then at Pax. "Sorry I was such lousy company on the way back."

He draped one arm over the back of her seat and leaned in close, giving her a seductive smile. "That's okay. I can think of ways we can make up for lost time."

Ellie's breath caught in her throat. He could literally charm the pants off of her, which thrilled and disturbed her all at the same time. But she'd promised herself that there would be no more hiding, so she shoved back any apprehension about falling for Pax. If she were in love with him—and she was very much afraid she was—she'd deal with it later. Today was about living in the moment. She closed the distance between them and kissed him with all the sensuality she could manage. When she broke the kiss, he seemed shaken, his mouth forming a slight frown.

Pax opened his door and got out without saying a word. Ellie worried that she'd done something wrong. He rounded the Jeep and opened her door. Then, he took her hand and helped her out. As he locked the doors, he led her along the path to the front entrance.

Ellie glanced back. "Shouldn't we get the cooler?"

Pax shook his head as he continued walking. "We'll get it later." His clipped tones made it obvious something had rattled him.

Once inside and up the stairs, Pax gently urged her along the hall until they reached her door. He let her unlock her door, and then he followed her inside. Pax relocked the door and leaned against it. His expression was troubled. Ellie wanted to erase those lines of worry from his beautiful features.

She reached to caress his cheek, and he grabbed her hand and held it. Pax gazed into her eyes, and this time, he saw the confusion on her face. He brought her hand to his mouth and kissed her open palm. Then, he tilted his head back against the door, closed his eyes, and shook his head in disbelief.

"Pax? Did I miss something?"

He pulled her to him. Then, he placed his hands on her hips and looked into her eyes. "Ellie…" Pax took a deep breath. "I don't know what you've done to me. I can't get you out of my head. I've never needed anyone as badly as I need you."

He swallowed hard. The kiss in the Jeep had shaken his foundation to its core. All Pax could think about was how he'd likely lose her when this was all over, and it scared him.

Ellie looked a little dejected. "Is wanting me such a bad thing?"

There was no way Pax could explain why his growing obsession with her was frightening—not without revealing the truth. It would be better if he kept his explanation vague.

"It's not a bad thing, Ellie. It's just a powerful thing." He felt her starting to pull away, and he tightened his grip. "I want you, Ellie. I want you all the time. Hell, I want you right now." Then, he kissed her, pouring everything he couldn't say into that one action.

Ellie broke the kiss and sighed. "I'm here. I'm yours. What are you waiting for?"

Without another word, he picked her up and carried her to the bedroom.

Outside, a man in dark clothing stood beside the building, a menthol cigarette hanging from his lips. He sneered and then crushed the cigarette under his boot, glaring up at the window he knew belonged to Elizabeth Manchester. He'd been watching them for months. That little whore was sleeping with her glorified babysitter, and he was sick of that muscle-bound moron always being in the way. He'd put a stop to both soon.

Monday morning at Manchester Aviation proved to be busier than normal. Pax spent every spare minute checking on Ellie through the video feed in her office. After the fourth time, he had to admit to himself that it wasn't just about making sure she was okay. He wanted to see her.

Lord, I have it bad. He was head over heels, and denying it didn't make it less true.

What he did with these feelings would be another matter entirely. He'd have to cross that bridge when he got there. Right now, he needed to focus on her safety.

Ms. Patricks wasn't at her desk, so Pax walked into Ted's office without knocking. He stopped short when he realized Ted wasn't alone. He recognized the gentleman, Harrison, from the first time he'd entered Ted's office months ago.

"Oh, so sorry, Ted. Didn't mean to interrupt. I need to talk to you." Glancing at Harrison, Pax continued, "I can come back when you aren't busy."

"No, it's fine, Pax. We were finished anyway." Ted stood up and shook Harrison's hand. "I'll talk to you later. I need to think about your proposal before I make a decision."

Harrison left the room without as much as a good-bye.

Once he was out of earshot, Pax sat on the edge of Ted's desk. "That guy seems like an odd one."

Ted chuckled. "Yeah, he can be. He has some ideas for a new design, but I'm not sure they are practical, so I'm going to have engineering take a look." Ted put some paperwork away in the top drawer and locked it. Then, he looked back up at Pax. "So, what do you have for me? Did that lead pan out?"

Pax was uncomfortable with sharing some things until he had facts to back them up. He carefully chose his words. "I'm very close to telling you who the blackmailer is. I'll have some concrete evidence in the next few days, if all goes as planned."

Ted leaned back in his desk chair. "Wow. You sound confident. It was that good of a lead, huh?"

Pax nodded. "I think a jury would find it pretty compelling."

Ted smiled. He stood and clapped Pax on the back. "Great work, Paxton! I knew you were the man for the job! We'll finally get this fiasco behind us, and Ellie's life can get back to normal."

Pax nodded but didn't reply otherwise.

Ted gave Pax a knowing smile. "Or maybe not completely back to normal. I think it's time she moved away from all the grief and sadness. She needs to find someone to share her life with, someone who'll make her happy again."

Pax's jaw clenched, but he still said nothing.

"Maybe you know someone we could set her up with?"

Again, he was silent, but Ted noticed that Pax was gripping the edge of the desk hard enough to turn his knuckles white.

Smiling wider, Ted commented, "Or maybe the person to make her happy is you."

Pax's eyes snapped to Ted's face.

"Don't fret, son. Anyone with eyes can see you have feelings for her. Honestly, I couldn't have handpicked a better man for her."

Pax didn't know how to respond. He wasn't sure he was ready to admit his feelings out loud, but he was sure that when he was ready to vocalize his love, Ellie should be the first to know. "I appreciate that, Ted. I'm honored you find me worthy, but—"

Ted interrupted, "Does she care for you, too?"

Pax shrugged. "I can honestly say I care for her as a dear friend, and I think she feels the same."

Sitting back down in his chair, Ted conceded, "I see. Well, I'm glad she has you as a friend as well as a protector. Hopefully, we can put this behind us soon."

Wanting to get this uncomfortable subject behind him, Pax agreed.

Ted walked to the office door and opened it, Pax following behind. He gave Pax another pat on the back. "It'll all work out great, thanks to you."

Exiting the office, Pax prayed Ted was right.

Without a doubt, Ted knew that Pax cared about Ellie very much. And if the clues he'd picked up on from Ellie were anything to go by, she cared about Pax, too. He smiled at the thought and then went back to returning missed calls from earlier in the day.

The next several days went by without incident.

Pax and Ellie had fallen into a routine they both enjoyed. They would take turns cooking for one other each evening, followed by a movie or TV, with Ellie curled up beside Pax in some fashion. He always spent the night, which Ellie loved, but she felt bad that he was paying for an apartment he was hardly ever in. Pax had assured Ellie it bothered her more than it bothered him, so she left it alone and accepted the gift of time he offered her.

She had no real clue where these feelings for him would lead or when it would end, but every time fear threatened to choke her, she would tamp it down. They avoided talking about commitment because it would complicate things. The last thing either of them needed was complications. So, Ellie enjoyed each day for what it was—one more day with the man who'd given her life back, the only man who'd ever gotten through to her.

Pax would occasionally spend a couple of hours or so at his apartment to give her alone time. He was more than happy to spend each night in her bed. In fact, he'd found he missed her quite a bit during the one time he tried to sleep in his own apartment. But he needed time to look for information about the handwriting samples, and it was difficult to do that with her around. She didn't know about the letters yet, and until Ted gave him the okay, Pax wasn't supposed tell her.

One Monday, Ellie had company most of the evening. Something exciting had happened to Nessa, and she'd claimed they needed some girl time, so she could give details to Ellie. Pax was glad for the excuse to slip across the hall and search through the box of Jacob's files again.

Throughout various documents, Jacob had made references to going on vacation, and it made no sense.

"Okay, Jacob, send me a little help. Why are you randomly talking about a vacation? How does this tie into anything at all?" Pax looked up at the ceiling. "I don't know if you're in heaven or what, but please send me something. I'm trying to keep her safe for you, Jacob." He chuckled to himself. "Man, I'm really losing it. I don't think I've ever been so desperate for answers that I resorted to talking to dead people." He sighed. "I'm not sure I've ever talked to myself quite so much either."

He glanced at Ellie and Nessa through the clock cam feed. He'd turned the sound down to give them privacy, so he couldn't hear their conversation, but it must have been something good. Nessa was excitedly waving her arms, and Ellie had a smile from ear to ear. He watched her for a few moments, smiling like an idiot, and then something caught his eye. To

Ellie's right, on the end table, was the photo of her on the beach from her last family vacation, the one they'd saved before the house caught on fire.

Pax jumped out of his chair and paced the room. *Could that be what Jacob was referring to?* There was something special about that photo. He prayed it was what he needed to figure out this mystery.

Nessa left Ellie's apartment shortly after eight p.m. She lightly skipped across the hall and knocked on Pax's door. When he answered, she gave him a huge grin. "Hey, hunky! Just wanted to let you know I was done with the girl stuff, so you can go over and spend some time making her extra happy." She gave him a wink.

Pax laughed. "Thanks for the heads-up."

Nessa placed a hand on his forearm. "Pax, seriously, thank you for making her so happy. I haven't seen her this free in…well, ever. That's because of you."

Pax looked a little embarrassed, but he was pleased to know Ellie's closest friend had seen the difference, too.

She walked down the hall but not before shooting a warning look at him and reminding him about their previous conversation. "Don't forget what I said about my talents with a meat cleaver though. That still stands. You hurt her, and I come after you."

He put his hands up. "I don't want her hurt any more than you do. I promise."

"Glad to hear it," said Nessa before descending the stairs.

Pax put some things away and crossed the hall to see Ellie. She was making a sandwich when he walked in.

She looked up and smiled. "Want one? I have enough to make two."

Pax shook his head and leaned against the breakfast bar. "No, thanks. I ate a little bit ago. How was your visit with Nessa? She seemed to be in a good mood."

Ellie threw her head back and laughed. "Oh, you don't know the half of it." Then, she licked some mustard off her finger and started putting away the ham and cheese.

Pax let his mind wander, thinking about her lips and fingers and tongue.

She caught him staring. "Hey, you still with me? You look far off."

He walked toward her and placed a kiss on her forehead. "I wasn't too far. I was just thinking about your bed." He kissed her nose. "And your naked body." He kissed her lips. "And my naked body." He kissed her neck. Then, he moved back up to whisper in her ear, "Those beautiful lips of yours make me crazy. And if I remember correctly, you rather appreciate my talents, too."

Ellie almost dropped her plate. "I'd say you are insatiable, but that would be the pot calling the kettle black."

Pax smiled into her neck as he continued to kiss and nibble his way back down. "I'm so glad I'm not the only one with this madness."

She sat the plate aside and ran her fingers through his hair. "Mmm…this is most definitely a madness. Think it's curable?"

Pax lifted her in his arms. "Lord, I hope not."

He smiled as he carried her to the sofa and sat down with her on his lap. He urgently kissed her and started unbuttoning her shirt. She ran her hands over his chest, searching for the edge of his T-shirt.

Pax pulled back. "Sorry. I should let you eat first."

Ellie pulled him close again. "I can eat later. Shut up and kiss me, you fool."

Pax gladly obliged.

The next morning was like any other. Pax had crossed the hall to shower and dress. Ellie did the same in her apartment, then fixed them a quick breakfast. Before they'd left that morning, Pax had stealthily grabbed the photo on her end table and slipped it in the briefcase he took to work.

Once he'd gotten to work, he'd closed himself up in the small office Ted had given him and begun to dismantle the frame. Just as he'd suspected, Jacob had written notes on the back of the photo, which were a list of seven numbers—all of them containing six digits. Those figures still hadn't quite make sense to Pax, but he did think the numbers looked vaguely familiar. His gut told him this was critical information. He just needed to figure out what they meant.

The day seemed to go well overall. Pax ran into Ted later in the afternoon, and noticed he was in a chipper mood. Pax attributed it to the fact that they were closing in on the enemy. Ted still didn't have a lot of information about the leads Pax had been chasing, but even without that facts, Ted seemed to have faith it would all be over soon. Pax fought his own mixed feelings on that. He wanted to be sure Ellie was safe, but he wasn't sure what the future would hold for them as a couple.

Pax worked all the way through lunch, occasionally checking on Ellie through the video feed. The next thing he knew, it was closing in on quitting time, and he still hadn't figured out Jacob's notes. The frustration was eating away at his patience. A knock on his office door jarred him from his current train of thought. He quickly stacked the papers into a discreet pile and invited the visitor in.

Ted opened the door and smiled at Pax. "Hey, sorry to bother you. I wanted to let you know I'm driving Ellie home a little early. I thought it was time I caught up with my girl." Noticing Pax's look of concern, he added, "It's something we used to do all the time. Little heart-to-heart talks while we got ice cream or something. Obviously, we aren't going for ice cream, but I want to see how she's doing, to connect with her. I promise not to leave her alone until you get there."

Pax smiled and nodded. "Sure thing. I'll see you in about an hour."

Pax spent another forty-five minutes muddling through the letters before he went home. Jacob had numbered the handwriting samples he sent to the lab to have them anonymously compared to the letters he'd been receiving. Those numbers had to somehow correspond to the numbers on the back of the photo, but Pax wasn't sure yet how or even why. *Why hadn't Jacob just put names beside the samples? Had he been afraid someone would see them?* Pax worried he was missing something important, something right under his nose.

13

Ted sat on Ellie's sofa, a glass of iced tea in one hand while he fidgeted with the other. Ellie moved to sit next to him, but she realized her photo from the beach was gone. Thinking it had fallen off the table, she placed her glass of tea on the coffee table and started to search for the photo on the floor.

"Everything okay, Ellie?" asked Ted.

She looked puzzled, but after not finding the photo, she sat down. "Yeah, everything is fine. I just misplaced something."

Ted looked down at his hands. Ellie hadn't yet noticed his nervousness, and he was struggling to hide it.

"Huh," said Ellie. "I have no idea where that photo went."

Ted looked back up at her. "A photo? Was it of you on the beach when you were little?"

Ellie's face registered surprise. Ted hadn't been in her apartment since she was almost kidnapped. *How had he known about the photo?* "Yes, that's the one."

Ted frowned and sighed. "Ellie, I need to admit something to you."

She looked at the man in front of her. He looked uneasy, and it made her uneasy as well. "What's going on, Ted?"

Ted set down his glass and turned to face her. "Pax has your photo. I saw it on his desk today."

Ellie was confused. "Why would he have my photo? That makes no sense at all."

Ted sighed and rubbed his temples. "He has it because he's trying to help me."

Ted leaned back into the cushions and continued to fidget. Ellie noticed his hair was graying. *When had Ted started aging?* She'd never noticed it until now. He looked tired.

"What is he helping you with?" Ellie felt her stomach turn. She knew she wouldn't like the answer Ted was about to give her.

He sat up again and looked her in the eyes. "You know how worried I was about you when your father died. I tried to leave it be, Ellie, but I couldn't. Pax is here, living across the hall and working at Manchester Aviation, because I hired him to protect you."

Ellie suddenly couldn't breathe. She could hear her heart beating loudly in her ears, and she felt as if it was going to burst forth from her chest. "What? He's what?" She heard her voice rise in a squeak of dismay.

Ted reached for her hands, but she pulled them away.

She stood, shaking with anger. "You hired a bodyguard specifically after I'd asked you not to?"

Ted stood as well and took a step forward. "Ellie, hear me out. I was worried. We had letters threatening your dad and then you. I had to keep you safe, and Pax has done a great job of it."

Tears welled in Ellie's eyes as she took in Ted's confession. "You lied to me, Ted. You and Pax both lied and deceived me. I know you had good intentions, but right now, I'm hurt, and I'm angry. I need you to leave."

"Ellie, please believe me when I say I was only looking out for you. The letters—"

Ellie interrupted him with a shout. "The letters! Why didn't you tell me about the damn letters, Ted? Did you think I was too messed up to handle it? Maybe you thought it would send me running back to my therapist in a fit of insanity? I don't know what you thought, Ted, but you were wrong. Now, get the hell out of my apartment!"

Ted walked slowly to the door, feeling defeated. Before he left, he turned to Ellie. "I know you'll eventually talk to me again, but please, don't take it out on Pax. He's a good man who was only doing his job."

Ellie didn't say a word. She just stared at Ted until he closed the door. Once Ted was gone, she let the tears flow down her face. *How dare he! How dare Ted do this to me behind my back!*

She felt like such a fool. Pax had been her bodyguard this whole time— not her lover or even her friend. He had been getting paid to spend time with her.

Damn, that hurt.

She felt her heart shatter into thousands of tiny shards. Pax's betrayal was more than she could endure.

She wrapped her arms around herself and paced her little living room, trying to decide how to deal with Pax. They couldn't continue to pretend. She would make it clear to him that she wasn't some birdbrained twit. She'd be calm and professional and let him know that he was fired and free to find his next assignment—preferably far, far away.

Ellie turned to pace once again, and out of the corner of her eye, she noticed the clock Pax had given her. In a fit of heartbroken rage, she picked it up and smashed it to the floor. Glass bits fragmented everywhere as well as some metal bits and springs. She felt a little better and wondered if she ought to break a few more things.

Looking around, she decided against it and went to get her dustpan and broom. Clearing away the larger pieces, she noticed something in the rubble that didn't look right. Picking up a small round object, she studied it and quickly discovered it was a tiny camera.

"That sneaky, deceitful bastard!" She angrily cleaned up the remaining pieces and put them in the trash, saving the camera for her inevitable confrontation with Pax.

About thirty minutes later, Pax pulled into his parking spot, still preoccupied with the numbers and what they might mean. As he got out of the Jeep, he noticed Ted's BMW was nowhere to be seen. Pax hurried into the building and took the stairs two at a time. Knocking on Ellie's door, he prayed she was home and okay. Ted was supposed to stay with her. *Were they together somewhere?*

The door opened a crack, and Pax saw Ellie's slight form. "Hey, beautiful. Can I come in?"

Ellie sucked in a deep breath. "I don't think that's a good idea, Pax. In fact, I don't think you should bother ever coming over again."

Pax frowned. She sounded like she'd been crying.

"What's wrong, Ellie? Are you okay? Please let me in." His voice expressed his urgency.

She opened the door and turned her back on him as she walked toward the middle of the room. He closed the door and came up behind her, wrapping his arms around her. She shrugged him off, put distance between them, and then turned around. Her eyes were puffy and red.

"Ellie, what happened? Tell me," Pax demanded.

Ellie let out a harsh laugh and then sniffled. "What happened? You happened, Tanner Paxton. You waltzed into my life and pretended to care about me just when I needed someone. You took advantage of my vulnerability and my loneliness, and I can never forgive you for that."

Pax's face grew angry. "What the hell are you talking about, Ellie? I did no such thing!"

"Oh, you didn't? Look me in the eyes, and tell me you aren't getting paid to watch out for me. Tell me you aren't here because you and Ted put together some carefully orchestrated plan. Tell me!"

Pax's face fell. *Oh Lord.* She knew.

"Ellie, I…I can't deny that I was hired to protect you."

She turned from him, and he saw her shoulders shaking. She was crying again. He'd never forgive himself for putting her through this pain.

"I'm sorry. I wanted to tell you, but I couldn't."

"You couldn't? Probably more like you wouldn't." She swiped the furious tears from her eyes. "So, was screwing me an added benefit? A little something on the side for good old Tanner Paxton while he killed time with the helpless, simpleton head case?" Her eyes blazed with anger and pain.

"No! Never!" Pax shouted. "I never used you, Ellie, not once. I was trying to keep my professional distance, but I couldn't help myself. If I remember correctly, you are the one who pushed us into sleeping together."

Ellie glared at him.

"But it doesn't matter who started it because we have something special, Ellie. You have to know that. I know you feel it."

Ellie stepped forward and slapped him. "What I know is that you are a liar. I feel nothing for you but contempt and disgust." She walked to the mantel, picked up the tiny camera, and handed it to him. "Take your lies and your damn pervert cam, and get the hell out of my life forever."

Pax looked down at the micro camera in his hand. He didn't know what to say to make her understand. "Ellie, please. Just let me explain."

She shook her head and pointed at the door. "Go, Tanner. Just go."

Pax's pain was building, his heart was breaking, and he didn't know how to make it stop. "Fine. Have it your way, Miss Manchester." He left, slamming the door. He thought he heard something hit the door behind him and break, but he just kept walking. He needed to think.

After walking around the complex several times, Pax spent the rest of the evening in his apartment, trying to solve the puzzle Ellie's dad had left behind. But he couldn't think clearly. Every time he closed his eyes, he would see Ellie's face. The pain in her eyes and voice haunted him. She was just so stubborn. If she'd only heard him out, maybe she'd understand.

Ted had warned him this would happen, but Pax really thought he could work it out with Ellie. *How had Ellie found out anyway?*

Pax tried to call Ted, but he wasn't answering his phone. Pax continued to pore over the documents before him until his bleary eyes could no longer focus properly.

The next morning, Pax drove to Manchester Aviation and went straight to Ted's office. His secretary was just settling in when Pax walked through the doors. She smiled and informed him that Mr. Bartley hadn't made it in yet. Pax walked past her and into Ted's office anyway. She'd spoken the truth. Ted wasn't in his office, and it didn't look like he'd been there since yesterday.

Pax was starting to get concerned about Ted as well. He passed back through the office, insisting she have Ted call him the minute he got in. Then, Pax went up to the third floor to see Ellie. He was disappointed to see that she was also not in her office. He tried calling her cell phone, but it went straight to voice mail. In a panic, he rushed out to his Jeep and drove back to her apartment.

Once there, he repeatedly banged on her door, but there was no answer. All was quiet inside. He didn't want to break her door down if he didn't have to, but he would if necessary. He needed to get inside her apartment. Pax ran down the stairs to the office of the superintendent. Mr. Baker was just finishing his breakfast and answered the door in a robe and slippers.

"Sorry to bother you, Mr. Baker, but I need you to open Elizabeth's apartment. I think she might be in trouble."

Mr. Baker's eyes went wide, and then he ran to get his key chain. He quickly scanned the keys until he found the one he was looking for. Just as he was handing it to Pax, Ellie and Nessa walked through the front door.

Mr. Baker looked at Pax with an annoyed expression. "She looks just fine to me, son." Then, he shut his door in Pax's face.

The noise attracted Ellie's attention, and she saw Pax. Her expression hardened, and Nessa followed her line of sight. Urging Ellie forward, Nessa headed straight for Pax. If her eyes were anything to judge by, she was planning to kill him right there in the entryway.

Pax held up his hands as she approached. "If you have that damn cleaver with you, I advise you keep it tucked away. I'm not in the mood."

Nessa poked his chest. "You're not in the mood? You broke her heart, you underhanded, two-faced jackass! I should end you now!"

Pax laughed bitterly. "I wish you would!"

That stopped Nessa in her tracks. She inspected him closer and noticed his five o'clock shadow and the circles under his eyes. He looked miserable. She sighed, realizing she kind of felt sorry for him. He had kept Ellie safe after all, so she supposed she at least owed him for that.

"We need to talk," said Nessa. "Meet me at Mattie's in an hour."

Pax nodded, and Nessa left him standing there as she went up to Ellie's apartment.

Roughly an hour later, Pax was sitting in a booth at Mattie's, wishing his glass were full of something stronger than tea. Nessa strolled in, located Pax, and marched toward him like a soldier heading into battle. Pax braced himself for the onslaught he suspected was about to be hurled at him. She dropped down in the seat opposite him and crossed her arms, staring him down.

Pax shook his head. "It's not the way it looks, Nessa, not even close."

"Why don't you enlighten me then? Because my best friend has spent the last several hours crying her eyes out over you." Nessa drummed her fingers along her biceps as she waited for Pax to explain.

"Ted hired me to keep her safe. That much is true. But I swear, our relationship was real. I care about her. I've never lied about that, not once. I just need her to listen to my side. I wanted to tell her the truth from the beginning, but Ted wouldn't allow it."

Pax placed his elbows on the table and rubbed his face with both hands. "Hell, this has become such a disaster. I was supposed to keep her safe while figuring out what was going on. I never intended to fall in love with her."

Nessa warily looked at him. "So, you really love her?"

Pax nodded. "I think I do. I've never felt like this about anyone." He sighed. "I don't know where our relationship was heading, Nessa, but we had agreed on no expectations for now. If Ellie truly doesn't want to see me anymore, then I'll respect her wishes. It'll hurt like hell, but I'll walk away. But first, we need to know who is after her. She still needs protection, and I can't do that if she won't let me near her."

Nessa looked doubtful. Pax needed Nessa on his side. It was the only way to get through to Ellie and convince her that she was vulnerable without him.

"Please, Nessa. Ellie is in serious danger. The person who wrote those letters isn't fooling around. The truck that almost hit her, the attempted kidnapping, the fire—none of it was accidental. Help me, so I can help her."

Looking him in the eyes, she nodded. "Okay, but no more keeping secrets. She deserves more respect than that."

Pax completely agreed.

After checking in at the office, Pax spent a good part of the afternoon working in his apartment. Ted hadn't come into the office at all, and Ellie was still across the hall, taking a personal day. He'd learned from Nessa that Ted was the one who had told Ellie. Ellie had thought it had something to do with a guilty conscience. *But why hadn't Ted warned me first or allowed me to be the one to explain?* Ted had known Pax's relationship with Ellie was becoming complicated. It didn't make sense that Ted wouldn't talk this out with Pax first, especially after all the times he'd practically begged Ted to let him tell her.

Pax pulled out the old letters found in Jacob's desk and then laid them out side by side next to the recent letters. They were similar, yet they weren't. Something about this whole situation nagged at him. Jacob had suspected someone close to his family. He'd had the handwriting analyzed. He'd hidden the identities of those samples, so only he could decipher them. Jacob hadn't wanted the blackmailer to know he was close to the truth.

Pax ran through a mental list of every potential suspect, even those he hadn't really considered a threat. The more he considered the possibilities, the more he worried. If his suspicion was correct, Ellie was in more danger than ever, and he had to get her to safety while he gathered evidence.

Picking up his cell, he called Nessa. "It's time. We have to do this now."

14

Ellie was trying to relax on the sofa, watching anything on TV that she hoped would take her mind off of Pax. Instead of forgetting about him, she found almost everything somehow reminded her of him. Even the stupid commercials brought him to mind—if only because it was something he'd make a smart-ass comment about.

Frustrated, she turned off the television and decided to read instead. She was pouring a glass of wine when she heard a knock on the door. Looking through the peephole, she saw Nessa on the other side and opened the door.

Nessa slipped in the door and closed it behind her. Then, she clicked the lock. Her face was ashen, and she had tears in her eyes.

Ellie rushed to her side. "Nessa, what's wrong?"

Shaking her head, Nessa calmed her breathing. "I promised myself I wouldn't cry."

Ellie put her arms around Nessa to comfort her and got a hard squeeze in return.

"I'm gonna miss you so much," Nessa said.

"What? Where are you going? You aren't making sense, Nessa. If you remember correctly, emotional mess is my job description. You're the levelheaded one." Ellie guided her to the sofa and sat close to her.

"I'm not leaving, Ellie. You are. You have to! It's just too dangerous to stay right now!" Another tear slid down Nessa's face.

Ellie's confusion turned into annoyance. "I love you, Nessa, but I'm not going anywhere. We've already discussed this."

Nessa grabbed Ellie's hands and gripped them so hard that it hurt her. "You have to listen to me, sweetie. You are in serious danger. I've seen the letters. I know what this psycho has threatened to do. You need to go somewhere safe."

Ellie wanted to be annoyed that Nessa had seen the letters before she had, but she couldn't get upset. Nessa was terrified. This was serious.

Ellie sighed. "Will I ever get to see these damn letters?"

Nessa nodded. "Of course, but you need to pack some essentials and get ready to hit the road."

Ellie's right eyebrow rose above the other. "And just where am I supposed to go?"

Nessa stood up and walked into the bedroom, so Ellie followed her. Nessa pulled a suitcase out of the closet and started tossing Ellie's underwear into it.

"Whoa, Nessa. Where am I going?"

Nessa put her hands on her hips. "A safe house."

A safe house? Am I under protective custody now?

She supposed Ted had set this up. He always tried to be a step ahead of the bad guy, especially when he had been on the force.

Nessa broke into Ellie's thoughts. "Please finish packing. We have to leave soon."

Ellie gave up. She knew there was no arguing with Nessa, and someone did seem to be hell-bent on destroying her, so the logical thing would be to go and hope this blew over soon. At least she'd be away from Pax. Maybe she'd have time to fortify her defenses before she saw him again.

"Fine. But I'm not loving this."

Nessa hugged her. "I just want you to be safe."

Once Ellie had packed the necessities, she put her suitcase in Nessa's Toyota Camry and climbed in. As they pulled out of the parking lot, Ellie couldn't help but look back at Pax's Jeep in its usual spot. As much as she didn't want to admit it, she missed him. Now, she was going to God knows where and might be gone a long time. He might move on before she got back. That should be a good thing, but the thought only made her feel deep loss.

A few minutes later, Nessa pulled into Mattie's and put her car in park.

Ellie looked more confused than ever. "Mattie's? Are we eating?"

Nessa got out and motioned for Ellie to follow. Once inside, they sat in a booth closest to the kitchen. Mattie came out and gave them water, and then she winked at Nessa and walked away.

Ellie rubbed her temples. "All this cloak and dagger is giving me a headache already."

Nessa gave her a faint smile and then checked her watch. They sipped water, not saying much of anything, mostly because Nessa kept shushing Ellie every time she'd tried to talk.

After about ten minutes, Nessa looked at her watch again and then stood up.

"I need to check my schedule, and Mattie wanted to ask you about catering that event for next month. C'mon." Then, she led the way through the kitchen toward the back office, with Ellie right behind her.

Once near the back office, Mattie stood up and gave Ellie a hug. "You'll be safe. Don't worry about us here. Don't try to make contact until you're given the okay, ya hear? They can find you."

Ellie felt completely lost. Everyone seemed to know what was going on, except for her. "Where am I going?"

Mattie and Nessa looked at one another. "We don't know. If we did, you wouldn't be safe."

Ellie started to protest when Nessa grabbed her arm and led her out the back door.

"You're leaving now. I'll stay to make it appear we're still inside." Nessa hugged Ellie one last time. "Stay safe, and do what you're told until the coast is clear. Promise me."

Ellie wanted to cry. This was happening too fast. "I don't know what is going on! I need more info before I leave you!"

Nessa took her by the shoulders and looked into her eyes. "Promise me."

Ellie let a tear fall. "I promise. I love you."

Nessa started to cry, too. "I love you, too, sweetie."

A silver GMC Yukon quickly pulled up to the back door, and Nessa turned Ellie around and pushed her into the backseat. As the SUV drove away, Ellie looked around her. Her suitcase was sitting in the seat beside her. She could only see the back of the driver's head, and it was dark.

"Hi, I'm Elizabeth Manchester."

The driver slightly turned his head, and she could make out his profile.

"Nice to meet you, Miss Manchester. Please let me know if I can make you comfortable in any way. We have a long drive ahead of us."

Ellie knew this man from somewhere, but she couldn't place him. "What's your name, if I'm allowed to ask?"

He chuckled. "Why wouldn't you be allowed to ask?"

She shrugged. "I don't know. I've never been whisked away to a safe house before. I'm not sure what the rules are."

He glanced back at her through the rearview mirror. "No rules really. You aren't a prisoner even though it might seem that way at first. But I do have to insist that you refrain from using your cell phone or anything that could potentially be tracked by GPS."

Ellie patted her pockets and realized she didn't even have her phone.

She sighed. "Not a problem, chief. My best friend is quite the pickpocket, and she stole my phone."

The driver smiled. "My name is Greg, by the way. Greg Matthews."

They talked casually as they drove. Once they were an hour away from town, Greg pulled off the highway and into a rest stop. He let Ellie stretch her legs, and then he escorted her to the restroom, standing guard outside the door. When they returned to the vehicle, he invited her to ride up front. She took him up on the offer and tried to quiz him about where they were going. Not surprisingly, he was tight-lipped on the location but assured her she'd be safe.

Ellie fell asleep right around the Oklahoma and Texas line. As they crossed into Texas, Greg picked up the burner cell phone he'd bought just for this purpose. He dialed a number that connected to another burner cell.

"Yeah, it's Greg. We're in Texas. See you in a few hours." He hung up and waited until they crossed a small bridge a couple of miles up the road. Once there, he stopped, rolled down the window, and tossed the phone into the river below.

Ellie woke up to soft '50s music playing in the background and sunlight shining in her face. Greg reached over and tried to adjust the sunshade, but it wasn't helping in her current position.

"Sorry. I was trying to keep it from bothering you."

Ellie stretched and sat up. "No problem. How long have we been driving?"

Greg looked at the clock on the dash and yawned. "About seven hours. We're almost there."

Ellie perked up and took note of the landscape flying by.

"Do you need to make a pit stop?" asked Greg. "We'll be at the safe house in another ten minutes or so, if you can wait."

Ellie stretched again. "No problem. I can wait."

She pretended not to be curious about their destination as she knew he wasn't going to tell her anything anyway. When they passed a city welcome sign for Jasper, Texas, she realized they really had driven quite a ways from home. She'd never been to Jasper, let alone Texas.

They continued to drive through to the outskirts of town, and then Greg made a left turn down a dirt road. They traveled a good five miles before he pulled into a gravel driveway that wound its way back into a large cropping of trees. He parked the SUV in front of a small brick farmhouse and got out.

Greg opened the door for her and helped her out. "Welcome to your temporary home, Miss Manchester."

She looked around her, taking note of how isolated the area was. Tired, but glad that they were no longer on the road, she thanked him. He retrieved her suitcase from the backseat and walked her to the front door. Unlocking it, he invited her inside.

The house was small but clean and in good condition. She tried to relax her shoulders as she set her case on the floor. She smiled up at Greg, attempting to look more optimistic than she felt.

"So...I guess you'll be staying here, too?"

Greg smiled back at her. "No, ma'am. You don't know me, and we don't want you to be uncomfortable. While I'd be honored to guard your safety, someone else is better suited for the job. I will be checking in now and then though."

Ellie had no idea who he was talking about.

"Ah, here he comes now," said Greg.

Ellie heard a door open behind her, and she spun on her heels to find Pax staring at her. He'd been towel-drying his hair, and he froze in his tracks upon seeing her.

Pax had known they were there. He'd seen the SUV pulling up. But he hadn't been prepared for the stab of pain caused by simply being in the same room with her. Her face told him all he needed to know. She wasn't even remotely ready to forgive him. She was unhappy and disagreeable, and it was all his fault.

"Hi, Ellie," he said softly.

She cleared her throat, struggling to find her voice. "Hi, Pax."

He didn't hear venom when she'd said his name, but with Greg standing there, Pax didn't expect her to chew him out either. He was sure she was saving that for when they would be alone.

Ellie didn't know if she should laugh or cry. Mere hours ago, she had lamented that she might never see Pax again, and all along, he'd been the one she was driving toward. Part of her wanted to hug him. Despite how angry she was with him, he was still trying to protect her. Another part of her wanted to slap him again for breaking her heart. The only way she was going to get out of this without more emotional scars was to keep this arrangement as professional as possible. She didn't want to be here, so she'd keep her distance and pray it would all be over soon.

Pax shook hands with Greg.

Ellie gasped. "You! You're the guy from the lake!"

Greg nodded. "Yes, ma'am. I met Pax there."

Ellie shot a glare at Pax. "Oh, good. More lies."

She grabbed her suitcase and stomped down the hall, tossing it and herself into the nearest vacant bedroom. Then, she slammed the door.

Greg chuckled.

"What's so damn funny?" Pax said, annoyed.

Greg raised his hands in surrender. "Don't get pissed at me. I told you keeping secrets from her was a bad idea."

Pax grumbled something about know-it-all old men as he entered the kitchen and started a pot of coffee.

Greg and Pax spent the next hour going over their plans. Pax shared his suspicions about the letters, and then they discussed various scenarios. Greg agreed that the perpetrator was likely someone still in Ellie's life and that it might even be more than one person.

Ellie sat on the back porch swing, next to the kitchen window. Greg and Pax were on the other side of the window, seated at a table, and discussing her safety. She felt like she was on the outside looking in, and all she could see was the mess that her life had become. It was shocking to think someone she knew, someone she possibly saw every day, wanted her dead. It boggled her mind. While she couldn't be happy about the circumstances, she was secretly pleased that she had Pax protecting her. They might not be lovers anymore, but she did feel safe with him.

The day passed slowly.

After lunch, Greg was getting ready to leave, and he promised Ellie he'd return in a day or so. She thanked him for his help and kindness and then kissed his cheek. Pax had never thought he'd be jealous of an older man, but for a fleeting moment, he wanted to be that aging cheek. He didn't know how he was going to survive being cooped up with her without going crazy. He'd probably need more cold showers. Thankfully, this part of Texas was a little warmer than Oklahoma in the fall.

As darkness fell, Ellie found Pax outside, sitting on the back steps. He was staring up at the stars, lost in thought. She sat next to him, careful to keep enough distance so that she couldn't touch him.

Pax glanced at her and then back up at the stars. "I love how quiet it is out here. We're far enough away that you can't hear traffic or neighbors or anything else. It's just us and nature."

Ellie looked up at the sky. "It is nice. You can see more stars compared to being in town."

Pax grinned at her. "Wait. It gets better."

He hopped up and ran into the house. He turned off all the lights, including the porch light, before walking back out the door. He let his eyes adjust a bit, and then he sat down next to her again. The moon was full and gave just the perfect amount of light.

After a few minutes, he pointed to the sky once more. "Now that your eyes have adjusted, look again."

Ellie stared into the night sky and found herself immersed in the inky blackness interrupted by thousands of beautiful tiny points of light. "It's breathtaking!"

Pax stared at her, not the sky. "It really is. It's the most breathtaking thing I've ever seen."

Ellie turned toward him and noticed he was looking at her. Whatever she was about to say caught in her throat. She'd been here for less than twenty-four hours, and he was already breaking down her walls again.

She was afraid to let him in. She wouldn't, not again.

Ellie grabbed the handrail and pulled herself to a standing position. She headed straight for the door, but Pax was already up and close on her heels.

"Ellie, we need to talk."

She turned to face him and put a hand on his chest. "No, I don't think we do, Pax. You were doing your job. I understand that."

He shook his head. "It's more than that, Ellie."

She shook her head in return. "Pax, what's done is done. Let's move forward."

Hope swelled in his heart just a little. *Maybe she was ready to pick up where they left off.* He moved to get closer, and she pushed him back, shaking her head.

"Not that kind of move forward. I meant, let's leave the past behind us and concentrate on what we are dealing with now—professionally."

Pax's heart shattered once again. He nodded his understanding and stepped back.

Ellie opened the door and moved inside. Then, she turned back and leaned against the doorjamb. "For what it's worth, Pax, if I have to be stuck here with anyone, I'm glad it's you. I know you'll keep me safe."

He looked at her and tried to smooth his expression. "I will. You have my word on it."

Ellie retreated to her room and prepared for bed, wondering how long she could continue to pretend she didn't care about him.

15

Ellie spent the next few days keeping herself busy with everyday tasks. She was the kind of person who would clean, go for a run, or throw herself into a major project when she needed to blow off nervous energy. Going for a run wasn't an option in this situation unless Pax went with her, which would defeat the purpose. There were no major projects to tackle either, so that left cleaning the safe house. It wasn't especially dirty, so she was just cleaning for the sake of killing time. Pax tried to convince her it was unnecessary, but she insisted. She needed to keep her mind off of everything, especially him. Much to her frustration, it hadn't taken long to clean such a small house.

She often found herself sitting on the porch swing, staring into the small forested area behind the house. Pax attempted to keep Ellie entertained, but her nerves were strained from his constant presence. She preferred to sit by herself and pretend she wasn't thinking about the man she was temporarily living with.

By the fourth day, Pax had grown frustrated with Ellie's lack of communication and constant cleaning. He needed her to talk to him. He needed to touch her. He needed…her.

After lunch, she was clearing the dishes away while Pax watched her from the kitchen table. Every time he'd offered to help, she'd shoo him away, so he sat there, watching her and feeling blessed and cursed at the same time.

Ellie was everything he could have ever asked for. When he'd first met her, it had been obvious that she was attractive. Then, he'd gotten to know her better and realized she had a beautiful heart and soul as well. She'd made him better. At the same time, losing her affection had all but broken him. He hadn't been sleeping well, and his appetite had been minimal. She was all he could think about. He knew this was a bad time to be brooding over losing her, but no matter how much he'd tried, he couldn't completely shove those feelings aside. They were always there, threatening to choke him. The idea of someone wanting to hurt this vibrant beautiful woman enraged him. Way too many complicated emotions were involved, and he needed to be more alert than ever.

Ellie was wiping down a countertop when Pax was struck with an idea.

"Ellie, have you ever taken self-defense classes?"

She stopped, turned to face him, and leaned against the counter. "No, I haven't." She let out a small self-deprecating laugh. "I guess that would have been the smart thing to do, considering all the crap that's happened to me." She sighed and tossed the dish towel on the counter.

Pax gave her a smile, the one he knew she struggled to resist. "It's never too late. I can teach you. It'd be a good way to make use of our time here, and it might come in handy at some point."

Ellie chewed her bottom lip while considering his proposal. This was actually a good idea. The house was too small to avoid him completely. Even when he wasn't in the same room with her, his presence seemed to linger. Learning a few self-defense moves would help her feel somewhat in control again—something she'd desperately needed to feel since fleeing home.

She nodded at Pax. "Yeah, that sounds like a good idea. When do we start?"

Pax stood up and put his hands in his pockets. He was optimistic and hopeful, but he kept his features calm. He hadn't really thought she would agree. "We can start this afternoon, if you'd like."

Roughly forty-five minutes later, Pax and Ellie were in the backyard.

He was teaching her how to throw a punch. "Power behind the hit is fine, but it's more important to hit target areas and take your opponent by surprise. Strike quickly, and be sure you keep your balance."

He held up his hands and let her practice hitting them. Ellie was a petite lady, but she had a decent amount of strength. Pax knew that the right training and a little practice would be a huge benefit for her. She'd be able to hold her own long enough to get away from her assailant.

He stood in front of her and showed her key striking points. "Go for the eyes, nose, throat, groin, or knees if possible."

Ellie warily eyed him. "The eyes?" The thought of blinding someone upset her a little.

He walked forward, took hold of her shoulders, and looked into her eyes. "Your attacker isn't going to play fair. You can't either. You do anything you can to get away. Anything."

She nodded, but he could tell she was struggling with the idea.

"Ellie, I mean it. You bite. You scream. You kick him in the balls. Scratch out his eyes. Slam the bridge of his nose. Do whatever it takes. Get him down, and then run."

She nodded more confidently, and he relaxed a bit.

They took a break, and Ellie got them each a glass of water. Sitting side by side on the large porch swing, they enjoyed the cooler temperatures and the tranquility.

Ellie was tired, but it was a good tired. She felt empowered by what little she'd learned already. She was also enjoying her time with Pax even though she wished it were otherwise. Maybe they could be friends again once this was all over.

She leaned her head back and closed her eyes. She wondered if it were possible for two people who had once been intimate to revert back to just being friends. She wasn't convinced it was possible. That was like knowing what chocolate had tasted like and then having it in front of you all the time but never getting another bite. She groaned and tried to think of something else.

Pax heard her throaty little groan. He loved all the sexy sounds she made even if she hadn't meant for them to be sexy. He had no idea what she was thinking about, but he hoped it involved him. Even if it was bad, at least she was thinking of him. There was always hope as long as he lingered in her mind somewhere.

Ellie stood up, stretched, and then turned to him. "I think I might take a power nap."

Pax smiled up at her, squinting a bit from the sun. He shielded his eyes with his hand. "Sounds like a good idea. Need any help? I've been told I make a good body pillow."

Ellie tried to calm the butterflies in her stomach. He was flirting with her again. She didn't know if he was being serious or just trying to break the tension between them. He winked at her and laughed. She fought the urge to throw something at him, but then she found herself laughing as well. It would be tough, but maybe they could be friends—in time.

She stood and carried her glass to the kitchen, placing it in the sink. As she walked toward her room, she hoped the image of using Pax for a body pillow wouldn't stay with her for long. If it did, she could kiss that nap good-bye.

When Ellie woke up, she felt refreshed, more so than she'd felt in several days.

While she'd been resting, Greg had come by with some supplies. He'd also brought some gun range targets, and Pax was busy fastening one to a hay bale not far from a small barn located to the left of the house. Ellie walked toward him when she spotted a brown leather wallet on the ground. Picking it up, she opened it to find Pax's driver's license.

She continued toward him, waving the wallet in front of her. "Hey, Batman. You dropped something."

Pax looked up to see what she'd meant. He rolled his eyes. "If I were Batman, that wallet would be much cooler and have secret gadgets attached to it."

She laughed as she handed it to him. Something slipped out just as he gripped the edge of the leather, and Ellie caught it. It was a photo of a younger Pax and a lovely young blonde woman.

Ellie arched an eyebrow at him, and in a singsong voice, she said, "Oh! Who is this?" She was curious and slightly jealous although she knew she had no right to be.

Pax reached for the photo, and she hid it behind her back. He grabbed Ellie and pulled her close, reaching behind her. She tried not to feel anything but amusement at this little game of keep-away.

She twisted around and said, "Oh no. You don't get it back until you tell me who she is!" Then, she slipped his grasp and jogged a few feet away.

"Ellie, please, just give me the photo." Pax looked a little irritated.

She was trying to have a little fun, and he was being a spoilsport. She didn't feel bad for annoying him a little. That was only a drop in the bucket compared to how she had felt during the last week.

Ellie shook her head again and repeated her demand, "Tell me who she is, and then you can have it back."

He started toward her again with an intense look on his face. Not thinking, she pulled the neck of her shirt out and stuck the picture in her bra. She realized too late that it had been a bad move. It wasn't a deterrent at all.

Pax's face changed from annoyed to downright sultry. "Oh, beautiful, you should know better than that. I'd be more than happy to remove your clothing to get what I want."

She had a feeling they weren't talking about the photo anymore. He continued toward her with determination in his eyes that caused her to panic. Ellie turned and ran into the house.

Pax swiftly but calmly marched toward her. Once he made it inside, he found her standing near the table, digging the photo out of her bra as quickly as she could.

Just as he reached her, she shoved the photo into his face. "Uncle!" she cried, hoping her surrender would appease him.

Without taking his eyes off her face, he deposited the photo into his pocket and then leaned into her. "Nope, that's not my uncle. And thank God, neither are you."

Then, he pulled her into him and kissed her.

She was caught off guard and gasped. He took that opportunity to tease her bottom lip with his tongue, and then he deepened the kiss. Despite all she'd told herself since learning the truth about him, she couldn't stop herself from kissing him back. She wanted him, and that wasn't likely to change even though her heart had a lot of healing to do.

Pax was in heaven. He'd been dying to kiss her for days. There had been times it was all he could do to keep his hands off of her. Now, she'd let her guard down and slipped back into the playful Ellie he had known before things went to hell. He wasn't about to let this opportunity pass. *Am I taking advantage? Absolutely.* And he wasn't a bit sorry. Deep down, he knew she cared for him, and he wouldn't walk away from her without a fight.

He pulled away from her lips and left a trail of kisses down her neck while simultaneously lifting her and setting her on the table. She buried her hands in his hair and made one of the throaty noises he loved so much. Pax slipped his hands under her shirt and rubbed his thumbs along her sides as he brought his lips back to hers. She kissed him back with an intensity that made him want to go full caveman on her and drag her back to his bed like some primal beast unable to restrain himself.

She pulled away from the kiss and looked up at him, her breath coming in short pants.

Pax grasped her chin in his hand and caressed her jawline. "Do you have any idea what you do to me?"

Ellie was overcome by so many emotions that she was unable to speak, so she just continued to stare at him while she tried to regain control of her breathing.

"Ellie, I know this might not be the right time, but I have to make you understand. Since the day I met you, my life has been crazy and chaotic and amazing. I don't want it any other way because that would mean you weren't in it. I don't want a life without you."

She blinked back a tear, and he gently kissed her lips again.

"You're not my client, Ellie. You're my will to live. I see you, and suddenly, my world is better. When I get close to you, all I can think about is touching you." Pax ran the backs of his fingers down her neck, lightly grazing her skin. "I want to make you feel what I feel when you smile at me. I want to hear your laugh and know I caused it. I would give up my last breath for you, Elizabeth Manchester. God help me, I'm in love with you, and nothing will ever change that."

Ellie wasn't sure what she'd expected Pax to say, but a declaration of love wasn't it. "You love me?"

Pax nuzzled her neck and then brought his lips to her ear. "I do. I love you so damn much it hurts. When you shut me out, I thought it would kill me. I don't think I can be happy without you, Ellie. I don't even want to try."

She smiled and pulled Pax closer as she hugged him. She was sure she loved him, too, but she wasn't quite ready to say it out loud. A part of her was still struggling with all that had happened between them.

At least I didn't catch him screwing an intern on his desk.

She kissed him again and sighed. "I need a little time, Pax. That's all."

He nodded. "That's fair. I can wait. You're worth whatever it takes."

She looked into his eyes and saw that he'd meant every word.

Then, he added, "That doesn't mean I'm not gonna try to cop a feel later when I'm teaching you how to handle a gun."

Ellie laughed. "I might just let you."

Pax grinned and decided this living situation could turn out to be pretty great after all.

He helped Ellie down and took her hand, leading her back outside to the target he'd been setting up.

Almost there, she pulled him to a stop. "I hate to bring this up again, Pax, but I really would like to know who the girl in the photo is."

He looked at her with a pained expression and then nodded. "Okay. Come sit."

They both sat on a hay bale, and he put her hand in his lap, palm up, looking at her delicate fingers. "I promised no more secrets, so I guess it's time I told you about her." He took a deep breath. "That's Carrie, Greg's daughter."

Ellie thought back to the blue-eyed blonde beauty. She could see the resemblance. The next question was a hard one, but she had to know. "Were you two an item?"

Pax traced the lines in her palm for a moment and then threaded his fingers through hers. "No. We were only friends, like siblings really. She passed away about eight years ago."

Ellie's heart broke for Pax. It was evident that this had been a tragic loss for him. "I'm so sorry. I shouldn't have pried."

Pax brought her hand to his lips, and he kissed it. "No, it's fine. It's time I told you what happened. And I'm hoping you asked because you were jealous. Were you?"

She blushed. "Yeah, I guess I was a little."

His smile widened. "I knew you liked me."

She gave him a small shove with her free hand, and he laughed.

Growing serious, he turned slightly toward her. "I've always had a rule never to get emotionally involved with anyone I'm protecting. It's dangerous. It leads to mistakes—sometimes fatal ones."

His expression was sad as he thought about it. "Greg is like a second father to me. He helped me turn my life around when I needed it most. Once I got out of juvie, he taught me how to use my fighting skills to protect others. So, I went to work for him in his security firm. Carrie worked with him, too. Her dad had taught her tactical defense from an early age, and she was good, really good. Together, we made a pretty good team."

Pax cleared his throat and continued, "One job we were working was particularly crazy. A wife was running from her abusive husband. Our job was to keep her out of harm's way until the assault trial. He was out on bail, but the system was failing her. She wouldn't feel safe until he was behind bars, and rightly so. He was a very dangerous man with a hair-trigger temper. Carrie and I were switching shifts late one night. Before she left, I confided in her about a relationship that had fallen apart. I wasn't in love with the girl, but at the time, the breakup really hurt." He smiled at Ellie. "She wasn't nearly as amazing as you are."

Ellie blushed again. "So, what happened next?"

Pax ran a hand through his hair and blew out a shaky breath. "I was upset and letting my emotions take over. Carrie was encouraging me to give myself time and then try again. She was great that way, always insisting I never give up until I found someone who could make me happy." He released a small laugh. "She would have loved you."

He continued, "So, anyway, she was trying to console me, and I was being an emotional idiot. While that was happening, this abusive jerk was sneaking in the back door of his wife's house. I heard a noise, and we both ran inside to find him standing in the living room, a gun in one hand and his wife in the other. He claimed he didn't want to hurt anyone and that he just wanted some time alone with her. We tried to negotiate for her freedom. In the end, Carrie was the one who got shot."

Pax's eyes filled with tears. "Hell, if I'd just been paying attention to work and not worried about some girl…" His words trailed off, and he wiped his eyes. "Anyway, I've never forgiven myself for that. In this line of work, emotions can be a dangerous distraction. It's why I worry about my feelings for you. Until all this is over, I should be keeping my distance. Instead, I'm trying to find excuses to touch you."

Ellie hugged Pax and then kissed him, hoping to ease some of the pain in his heart. "It'll all work out fine, Pax. I know it."

He wrapped his arms around her and held on tight. Target practice could wait.

16

Ted walked into his office, flustered and worried. Everything seemed to be falling apart. He thought back to five days before. After telling Ellie the truth about Pax, she had done just what he'd expected her to do. She was livid. He wasn't sure how Pax was holding up, considering Ted hadn't talked to him in days. He probably should have given Pax fair warning about Ellie, but it had just seemed like the best time to tell her.

After leaving her apartment, Ted had decided he needed a few days off. He'd been working so hard, and the stress had been getting to him. He'd spent three days at his favorite getaway, trying to leave the world behind for a bit. When he had come back, he'd felt more like his old self.

Two days ago he had gone to Ellie's to apologize, but she'd never answered the door. He'd decided to visit Pax, but he hadn't been home either. He'd tried again the next day with no response or appearance at work from either, so he had begun to worry.

In his office, Ted called the only other person that might have some insight.

"Hey, Nessa. It's Ted. Have you heard from Ellie?"

"No, she's not allowed to use the phone, remember?"

Ted frowned. *She can't use the phone?* "Excuse me?"

Nessa sighed. "Remember? Pax said she couldn't use anything that could be tracked."

"Nessa, Pax didn't tell me anything. I don't know what's going on."

Nessa became worried. "You didn't work this out with Pax? I thought this was your plan."

"No," sighed Ted. "It's not my plan. Did he say where they were going?"

"No, he didn't. Pax said it'd be too dangerous if I knew. I just assumed since you hired him...I guess I just assumed too much." Nessa fought down the urge to panic. "Will she be okay, Ted?"

"I'm sure she'll be fine. Pax cares about her. He'll keep her safe."

"Okay. Keep me posted, please."

"Will do, kiddo." Ted hung up and rubbed his temples.

Why hadn't Pax told me they were running off? This wasn't good.

He knew Ellie was mad at them both, and he knew Pax was in love with her, but he'd never expected this. Something had gone horribly wrong if Pax took Ellie out of town without telling him.

Shaking his head in disbelief, he picked up his phone again and called a friend of his at the police department. "Hey, Barnes. We need to talk. I think Ellie's been kidnapped."

In less than an hour, Ted had driven to the police department and had given a full report to Detective Barnes, and he was wringing his hands with worry. "I dunno, Barnes. I thought I was doing the right thing in hiring Paxton. He genuinely seemed like a great guy. But they grew close, and I started to worry that he was becoming obsessed with her."

Detective Barnes put out a cigarette and shuffled the papers in front of him. "Are you sure she didn't willingly go with him, Ted? It's not uncommon for couples to feel impulsive and run off together."

Ted shifted in his seat. "I considered that, but that's just not Ellie's style. Besides, she was very angry with us both for lying to her. And Nessa said that Pax told her no one could know where they were going. He's not even letting her call anyone because the calls could be traced back to their location." Ted leaned forward. "I know it could all be legit, Barnes, but I'm worried. I just want to be sure this was done with her consent."

Barnes nodded. "Okay, Ted. We don't have any evidence, outside of your gut feelings and her friend saying this guy took her to a secret location. But I'll put the word out on them and on the vehicle Nessa said they had left in. Maybe someone has seen something, and then we can verify that Ellie's safe."

Two days later after Ted had reported them missing, Pax and Ellie sat in the tiny living room of the safe house. She'd finally gathered the courage to read the threats she'd been receiving. Pax sat close to her, ready for any emotional reaction she might have. She was certainly shocked but also confused.

"Pax, I have no idea who would have blackmailed my father. Now, I do wonder if it had something to do with my mother and the reason she was murdered." She swallowed the lump in her throat. "Maybe this is the same guy." Reaching the more recent letters, she frowned. "I'm not sure what I have to do with it though. How have I ruined someone's life? I don't get it."

Pax didn't either. There was just too much here that didn't properly mesh together.

126

He handed her the photo and showed her the numbers on the back. "Do any of these numbers make sense to you? Do they look familiar in any way?"

Ellie studied them for a moment, and then her face brightened with recognition. "Oh! I know these. I think they're employee ID numbers."

Pax looked at them again. "Are you sure?"

Ellie took a sip of her coffee and nodded. "Yes, I'm positive."

Pax got a sick feeling in the pit of his stomach as he took in the possibility that his earlier suspicions were correct. It was someone they worked with. Jacob had suspected it all along, but he hadn't lived long enough to reveal the truth.

Pax made notes on a scrap of paper. "I'll see if I can match these up somehow."

Ellie twisted a lock of hair around her finger. "Maybe we should call Ted. He could give us the info we need."

Pax frowned. "We can't really trust anyone at this point, Ellie."

She tried to understand, but it all seemed so ludicrous. "Pax, this is Ted we're talking about here."

Pax stared down at the numbers in his hand. "There's no telling who's watching or listening."

Ellie was confused, but she trusted Pax, so she didn't push the issue further.

Greg arrived with more supplies, and shortly thereafter, he took Ellie out back to continue her self-defense training. They'd hung a punching bag off of a large limb, and Ellie was working it over. Greg was incredibly proud of how much she'd learned in such a short time.

As she swung her fists at the bag, she asked him, "So, why did you get into the security business?"

Greg shrugged. "Honestly, I saw a need, and I filled it." He kicked a rock away with his boot. "The police do the best they can, but their hands are tied most of the time. People need help to prevent the attacks, so that's what we do. When the fears and threats are real, we step in."

She stopped and wiped the sweat from her brow. "Makes sense. Pax told me how you took him in...and about Carrie." She looked him in the eyes then. "I'm so very sorry."

Greg gave her a sad smile. "I miss her every day, but she wouldn't have changed what happened because she was defending the defenseless. And she wouldn't have blamed Pax either."

Ellie understood what he was saying. She also understood blaming yourself since that was pretty much all she'd done since her mother died.

Greg handed her a towel. "He's a good guy, you know. A little damaged but nothing a whole lot of you couldn't fix."

Ellie wasn't sure how to respond to that, so she just smiled.

Greg continued, "You make him happy, Ellie—happier than I've seen him in years."

Ellie laughed. "That serious sourpuss in there is him being happy?"

He chuckled. "Not exactly. That's him being worried about the woman he loves. But all those little moments—when he smiles at the mention of your name or when you walk into a room—is what he'd be like all the time once this threat is neutralized."

Ellie added this information to all the other things she'd learned about Pax since she met him. He was a complex man, but she was starting to believe he would be very much worth any obstacles they might face along the way.

Inside, Pax looked through the handwriting samples and managed to match up two of them, thanks to a couple of forms he'd found among the various bits of information. Jacob had written the numbers in reverse order just to make it a bit more difficult to decipher. It wasn't terribly original or clever, but it had kept Pax stumped for quite a while. If Ellie hadn't realized they were employee ID numbers, he might still be pulling out his hair over them. The two that matched were both clean. He didn't need to figure them all out. He just needed to match one sample to the letters.

Ellie came in from her workout feeling tired but confident.

Greg smiled at her and nodded to Pax. "Now, if he gets out of line, you can kick his ass."

Pax had his back turned to them. "Hey, old man. Just because I'm not looking at you doesn't mean I can't hear you."

Greg laughed. "I'm telling you, man. She can probably take you."

Ellie laughed as well. "Yeah, maybe I can."

Pax hid a small smile and tilted his water bottle back, taking a deep drink. He wiped his mouth and replied, "I greatly look forward to her trying."

Greg rolled his eyes. "Trust you to turn this into something sexual."

Ellie blushed, but she privately admitted she was thinking pretty much the same thing.

"Well, I'd better get going. You guys have fun. I'll see you in a couple of days unless you figure more out between now and then." Greg tipped his black ball cap in Ellie's direction. "Miss Ellie, always a pleasure." Walking past Pax, he said, "Dirtbag, be nice to her." And then, he was gone.

Ellie walked past Pax as she headed down the hall. "I'm gonna get in the shower. I feel grimy."

Pax temporarily let his imagination wander to the shared bathroom. He'd really love to join her, but he wasn't sure she was ready for that yet. He didn't want to push her. And he really needed to keep working anyway. "Sure thing. I'm gonna keep at this. I think I'm close." He heard the bathroom door shut, and he went back to concentrating on the letters.

Within about twenty minutes, Pax had found two more documents with employee ID numbers and had figured out the mystery handwriting sample. It was hard to believe, but there it was, hard proof, before him. He rubbed his face and stared at the page again.

"Damn. Just…damn!" His anger flared, and he threw an empty ashtray that was sitting on the coffee table. It hit the wall and made a dent in the sheet rock. Standing, Pax started pacing the tiny living room.

Ellie emerged from the bathroom, wrapped in a towel. "Everything okay? I thought I heard something break."

Pax took the few steps necessary to reach her, and then he placed his hands in her damp hair and kissed her as if he hadn't seen her in years. Ellie was surprised by the emotion that seemed to emanate from his touch.

Breathless, she asked, "What was that for?"

He blinked a couple of times and then let go of her. "I'm sorry. I don't mean to rush you."

She reached forward and pulled his head down to hers. "I don't see a reason we can't kiss now and then, do you?" This time, she was the one to close the distance between them.

The next afternoon, Pax was out in the driveway, working on the blue 1980 Ford Bronco they'd bought when they got rid of the SUV. Greg was talking to him while he replaced the plugs and wires. Pax shared his previous night's findings with Greg as he worked.

"Are you sure, Pax? Absolutely sure?"

Pax nodded. "Yeah, I'm sure. I haven't told her yet. I don't know how."

Greg frowned. At that moment, Ellie came out in blue jeans, a flannel shirt, and tennis shoes. Her hair was pulled up in a messy arrangement on top of her head. Pax figured she'd probably just grabbed a clip, twisted it up, and walked out the door, and he thought she was easily the most beautiful creature in existence.

"What are you fellas working on now?"

Pax held up a spark plug. "We just replaced these. Looks like we're gonna need to change the fan belt and filters, too."

Ellie's face grew hopeful. "By any chance, will you be going into town for the parts?"

He caught the enthusiasm in her voice. "Sorry, Ellie. We can't take you into town." Then, he turned back to work on the truck.

She groaned. "Please, Pax. I'm going stir-crazy here!"

He glanced back at her. "I know, but I'm not sure it's a good idea."

Greg gave Pax a little shove. "C'mon, man. Take her to pick up the parts. It shouldn't be a problem."

Pax looked at Greg like he'd lost his mind.

Greg continued, "I'll stay here and tune that old motorcycle in the back while you guys make the run. You can cheer the little lady up. She needs some happy moments in all this chaos."

Ellie gave Pax a look that melted his resolve.

He sighed. "Okay, but we can't stay in town long. Got it?"

She jumped up and down and hugged Greg. Then, she grabbed Pax to kiss him, but he stopped her.

"Whoa! You're gonna get all dirty," Pax said.

She didn't care, so she kissed him anyway, then wrapped her arms around him in a big hug.

He hugged her back, and over her head, he saw Greg mouth, *Sucker.*

Pax flipped him off, and Greg laughed.

An hour later, Pax had changed, and they were in the Bronco, on their way into Jasper. Pax was enjoying listening to Ellie's excited chatter about the horses she'd seen on the way out. He was just about to ask her if she'd like a horse of her own when everything suddenly turned into a horrifying slow-motion sequence.

There was a loud sickening crunching sound, and the landscape around them was spinning. The Bronco rolled a couple of times, landed on its top, and slid across the pavement. It took Pax a moment to realize that they'd been hit by another vehicle. His head was beginning to pound, and he was hanging upside down from his seat belt.

He looked over to check on Ellie. She was hanging from her belt as well, but she was out cold.

Pax reached out to touch her. "Ellie? C'mon, talk to me, beautiful. Wake up."

She groaned a little but didn't open her eyes. Then, he saw the blood dripping from her scalp. She had fragments of glass in her hair.

He tried to get his seat belt unbuckled, but it was stuck. He jerked on the strap, but still, nothing happened. Two arms reached inside the busted-out window on Ellie's side of the vehicle and supported her body while another arm reached in and unbuckled her. Then, the arms pulled her through the window.

"Hey!" yelled Pax. "Help me out of here."

He had to make sure Ellie was okay, and Pax had no idea who was out there. He saw a pair of booted legs come to his side of the truck, and then the man bent down.

"Fancy seeing you here, Paxton."

Pax didn't know if he was seeing things or if the man crouching before him was real. "Harrison?"

The large man smiled at him. "In the flesh. Now, you just stay here like a good boy while we take Miss Manchester back to where she belongs."

Pax struggled to get free, and Harrison frowned.

"Now, now, none of that, Paxton. We can't have you getting loose and messing things up once again."

Harrison stood up and pried opened Pax's door. Then, Harrison kicked Pax in the head, knocking him out.

17

Ellie opened her eyes and rapidly blinked them. She struggled to adjust to the darkness. A minuscule amount of light was coming from somewhere to her right, but it didn't illuminate enough for her to immediately recognize her surroundings. She smelled the familiar scent of menthol cigarettes. *Marcus smoked menthols.* Confused, she tried to sit up, and she realized she was in the backseat of a car, her hands were tied together at her back, and her head hurt.

"Hello, sleepyhead."

Ellie froze. *It is Marcus! Why am I with Marcus?* She felt sick to her stomach. "Where am I?"

Marcus smiled. "You're safe now."

What? This makes no sense. As her head began to clear, she started to remember. She had been in the Bronco with Pax, and then things had gone crazy. "Where's Pax? Is he okay?" Her voice was panicked.

Marcus scoffed at the mention of Pax's name. "You don't need him, Ellie. You need me."

She fought down the dismay that threatened to overtake her. Marcus had lost his marbles, and Pax might be hurt or dead.

Marcus pulled the car through a small patch of trees and parked. "Time to get out, sweetheart."

She had to bite her tongue to keep from snapping at him. Provoking him would only make things worse. Ellie needed to stay calm until she could figure out how to get away.

Marcus helped her out of the backseat and then took her upper arm before leading her down a path. It was dark, and Marcus was using his other hand to hold a flashlight. After walking for a few minutes, they came to a clearing and a little cabin. Ellie recognized it as the cabin Ted owned and frequented when he wanted to get away from everything. They were back in Oklahoma. The cozy little getaway was located on a private plot of land about eighty miles from home. He'd loaned it to her and Marcus one week during the summer, shortly before they'd broken up.

Marcus pushed open the door and pulled her in behind him. He sat her on a nearby small bench. Then, he shut and bolted the one tiny lock the door had. Turning to Ellie, he smiled and brushed his fingers over her cheek.

"Remember the week we spent here, Elizabeth? That was probably the best week of my life." He lifted her to her feet and turned her around. Then, he untied her hands.

Ellie instinctively rubbed her wrists, and Marcus frowned.

"I'm so sorry, sweetheart. I told that big oaf we didn't need to tie you up, but he seemed less sure you'd come willingly."

He took one of her hands and led her to the large bed near the fireplace. He motioned for her to take a seat, and then he set to work on getting a fire started. Ellie looked around the small one-room cabin. There was a back door not far from the bathroom, but she'd have to run past Marcus to get to it. She needed to bide her time while she figured out what to do.

Once the fire had roared to life, Marcus sat down beside her on the bed. "Now, that's more like it." He pressed a kiss to her cheek. "Isn't this romantic, darling?" Then, he moved to kiss her ear and neck.

She was revolted, but she fought the urge to recoil at his touch. She needed him to trust her. She had to catch him off guard at the right time—just like Pax had taught her. Once Marcus's hands started to wander, she couldn't take it anymore, and she pushed him away.

"Please, Marcus, can I have a little time to relax first? It's been a rough day, and I could use a drink."

Marcus seemed suspicious, so she ran a finger down his arm and leaned in close.

"You know me. I like to loosen up a bit first." She winked at him, hoping she was mimicking the demeanor he expected.

He smiled at her and then closed the gap. He brushed a brief kiss across her lips. "Sure, sweetheart. I picked up something special just for this occasion." He walked toward the small kitchenette and pulled a bottle of champagne out of the fridge. Taking two coffee mugs from the cabinet, he filled each one with the bubbly liquid. "I'm sorry this is a little primitive. I didn't have as much time to prepare as I thought I would."

Ellie faked a smile. "Don't give it another thought. This is perfect."

Marcus brought over the drinks and handed one to her. They clinked mugs, and Marcus gulped his down. Ellie sipped at hers and prayed Marcus would drink most of the bottle. He was always a lightweight, and it would be easier to get away if he were tipsy.

Marcus stood to get a refill, and Ellie quietly poured hers into a small planter sitting next to the bed. Whatever had been planted in there was long dead, but thankfully, there was just enough dirt to soak up the liquid without making a sound. Marcus turned around just as Ellie was pretending to drink the last drop. She smiled at him and motioned that she needed more.

Marcus brought the bottle over to the bed and filled her cup again. She continued to pretend to drink and tried to keep Marcus talking. Her nervous energy was building to the point that she could hardly sit still. It occurred to her that she might be able to use that to her advantage.

"Mind if we go for a walk? Being cramped up in that car for so long after the accident has made me kinda stiff." She stood and placed a hand on his shoulder. "Besides, the clear night sky is gorgeous this time of year. Plus, it's cool out. It might be fun to make out under the stars."

Marcus was so deluded and desperate for her to want him that he never questioned her motives. "Sounds nice. Honestly though, I'd rather just stay here on this bed."

Ellie took his hand. "Please? We could stop at that little clearing where we found all those wildflowers and lay down a blanket."

Marcus sighed and rolled his eyes. "I guess. But you're staying close to me." His tone told Ellie that he wasn't completely off guard despite the champagne.

He grabbed the blanket off the bed and tucked it under one arm. Then, he unlocked the door and led her outside. She struggled not to shiver from the cool air. If Marcus noticed she was cold, he'd insist they go back indoors. He tightly grasped Ellie's hand and impatiently pulled her along behind him.

She struggled to keep up with his pace. "Can we slow down? I'm about to trip over my own feet."

His annoyance at her slower gait was obvious, but he minimized his steps a little to give her time to catch up. Once they reached the clearing, she searched the ground for the perfect spot. Taking the blanket from Marcus, Ellie spread it out near one edge of the tree line and sat down. When she patted the spot to her right, he sat next to her. He tried to pull her close, but she playfully swatted him away and laughed.

"You always were so impatient. Let's enjoy the view for a few minutes first," she said.

Lying down on her back, she pretended to gaze up at the stars. For just a moment, she was taken back to the little porch in Texas with Pax sitting so close, showing her the beauty of the universe beyond them. She closed her eyes and prayed that he was okay. Whatever happened to her, she could bear it if Pax were safe.

Marcus saw her closed her eyes, and he jumped at the opportunity to grope her. Her eyes flew open as he ran a hand up her thigh. His face was hovering over hers, his lips mere inches away. She spread her left arm out to one side, pretending to stretch. Marcus smiled at what he perceived to be total submission and kissed her. While he forced his tongue into her mouth, her left hand was frantically searching for any object she could use as a weapon. Finding a large rock, she firmly grasped it. She ended the kiss, and as she did so, she brought the rock up and smashed it into the side of Marcus's head with all the force she could muster.

Marcus made a loud grunting sound and rolled off of her, holding the side of his face. Ellie quickly scrambled to her feet and ran into the trees. She wasn't sure where she was going, but she knew she would be better off lost out here in the woods than with Marcus. She'd rather die of the elements than be forced to live as Marcus's captive.

Ellie ran until she couldn't run anymore. Her lungs burned, and the cool air was starting to numb her extremities. She listened for any sounds that indicated he had followed her, but for the time being, she heard nothing. Slowly and carefully, she walked toward an area full of brush and bushes, doing her best not to make any noise. Once there, she looked for a place to safely rest. After she'd moved some of the brush, Ellie crawled back in between a couple of bushes, praying they would make decent cover. She'd just gotten settled when she heard it.

"Elizabeth! Where are you? Come out, come out, wherever you are!"

She wrapped her arms around her knees and tried to make herself as small as possible. His voice was coming closer, and it took all her willpower not to panic. Marcus's boots came into view, and she bit down on her lip to keep from gasping out loud. He was less than two feet from her.

He stood still, listening. "I know you're here somewhere! Come back to me, so we can talk, sweetheart!" He stopped to listen again, but he heard nothing, except for the sounds of nature. He kicked a large stick out of his way, and it smacked the bush in front of her.

"It's him, isn't it? That Paxton guy? You don't love me because of him." Marcus was no longer yelling. He was just talking to her. He had to know she was hiding nearby. "I'm not a fool, Elizabeth. I know you were sleeping with him. I've been watching you." His voice was eerily calm. "Harrison saw you two all cozied up together several times as well."

Marcus crouched down and picked up a leaf, tearing it to shreds. "If only you had come with me when I tried to take you, we'd be happy together, living in Mexico or on some beautiful island. But no, you had to fight. You had to trip us both. Then, that muscle-bound pretty-boy came out and ruined everything." He tossed the leaf's remains on the ground. "I sent you letters, Ellie. I don't know if you ever got them. I'll admit to threatening you, but I never really meant it. I just wanted you back."

Ellie struggled once again to keep her fear at bay. Her legs were starting to cramp, and she needed to move them, but she wouldn't dare try with him so close.

Marcus stood there for a few minutes longer. Then, he made a huffing sound and continued walking in the opposite direction from where he'd started.

Ellie waited until she could no longer hear the twigs breaking under his shoes. Then, she stretched out her legs and softly groaned. She was really getting cold. Waiting a few moments more, she cautiously climbed out of the bushes and stood up. Stretching, she tried to decide what to do next. Ellie stepped around the large mass of bushes and trees, searching for any indication of civilization—or at least, another cabin.

She was still trying to determine which direction to go when she saw a flashlight in the distance. She hid herself behind a large tree and watched as the light got closer. Once close enough to see, she realized who it was. "Ted?"

Surprised, he jumped back and turned the flashlight toward her. "Ellie? Is that you?"

Ted's come to save me! She ran toward him and pulled him into an embrace.

Ted hugged her back. "Oh, Ellie, I'm so happy to see you!" He pulled back and looked at her. "Where's your jacket? You're freezing!" He pulled off his own coat and wrapped her up in it. "C'mon, buttercup. Let's get you warmed up."

The cabin wasn't all that far, and once they reached it, Ted put her in front of the fireplace. He added a couple of logs to keep it going and then made her a cup of coffee. "How did you get here?"

Ellie pushed her fingers toward the flames, hoping she'd regain feeling soon. "It's Marcus. He's deranged and dangerous. There was an accident, and then I woke up in Marcus's car just before we got here." She choked back the urge to cry. "I think Pax was hurt."

She gave herself a moment to calm down before she continued, "Marcus admitted to writing some of those letters and to trying to kidnap me at the flea market." Suddenly, it occurred to her that Marcus would probably try to come back after giving up his search for her. "Ted, please tell me you have a gun or something on you. I'm scared of him."

Ted handed her the cup of coffee and sat next to her. Patting her on the leg, he said, "No worries. I'll take care of Marcus."

She leaned against Ted and smiled. "Thank you. I know I was angry, but I owe you an apology. Pax really has kept me safe. I don't know what happened to him after I was taken." She fought back fresh tears. "I hope he's okay."

Once again, Ted tried to comfort her. "You just worry about warming up. I'll see what I can learn about Pax, too."

She wiped her eyes and hugged him. "You're the best." Then, she started sipping her coffee, enjoying the warmth it gave as she drank.

While Ellie recuperated, Ted made a phone call. "Hey, it's me. Do you know anything about Tanner Paxton?"

Silence filled the room as Ellie held her breath, praying for good news.

"Okay. Let me know if you learn anything. Thanks."

Ted hung up the phone and gave her a reassuring smile. "I'm sure he's fine. He's a tough guy. Don't worry your pretty little head about him, okay?"

Moments later, the door opened, and Marcus walked in. Blood was caked on the right side of his face and hair. When he saw Ted, he froze. Uneasy, he looked around. "What are you doing here?"

Ted stood up and glowered at Marcus. "In case you've forgotten, I own this cabin. What are you doing here?" He gestured toward Ellie. "What have you done?"

Marcus shifted nervously. His gaze flittered back and forth between Ellie and Ted, and then he cleared his throat. "I just wanted to spend time with her, like we used to."

Ted walked toward a duffel bag sitting on the counter. Unzipping it, he pulled out a gun. "Marcus, you know you aren't supposed to be here."

Marcus took a shaky step back. "I'm sorry. It's just…I just wanted to be with her again. Keeping her alive wasn't part of the plan, but I couldn't kill her. I wanted her too much."

Ellie pulled the jacket around her a little tighter and looked between the two men, trying to understand the odd conversation they were having.

Ted sighed. "I know, Marcus. She has always been your biggest weakness." He motioned for Marcus to come closer. "It's okay, son. I forgive you."

Marcus smiled a bit and took a few steps forward. Then, he hugged Ted. "I'm sorry, Pop. I just couldn't do it."

Ted gave him a slight squeeze and said, "It's not a problem anymore, boy." Then, he stuck the gun in Marcus's chest and pulled the trigger.

18

When Pax came to, he was on a stretcher in the back of an ambulance. Greg was wiping blood off of Pax's face and inspecting a nasty bruise on his head. An EMT was checking Pax's vitals while a police officer waited nearby, ready to ask questions about the accident.

Pax refused to let them take him to the hospital and insisted Greg get him out of the ambulance. Pax spent a few minutes giving his statement to the officer. He never saw the other vehicle, but from the looks of the site, they had been rammed by a beat-up green Chevy, which now sat abandoned on the side of the road. Upon closer inspection, Pax realized it was the same truck that had almost run Ellie down after they first met.

He grabbed Greg. "Ellie's been taken! We have to find her now!"

Greg nodded and walked toward the police car to talk with the officer. A few minutes later, Pax climbed into Greg's rental car, and they headed back to the safe house. Pax was fidgeting. Greg gave him a sidelong glance. "You need to calm down Pax."

Pax shot him a frustrated look. "We need to hurry, Greg. I don't know how much time we have before they hurt her, if they haven't already."

Greg shook his head. "You can't think that way, Pax. They're probably taking her back to Oklahoma, so we have time to catch up to them, if we can just figure out exactly where the hell they took her."

Pax swallowed a lump in his throat. "Yeah, I hope so."

Once they pulled into the driveway, Pax and Greg both ran into the house, quickly packing up anything they might need. Pax was mostly concerned about having his gun and plenty of ammo. He felt sure there would be no peaceful negotiation for Ellie, not after all the work they'd gone through to get to her.

Loaded and ready to go, Pax and Greg headed north, back into Oklahoma. Greg had made a lot of contacts over the years and had friends in just about every agency, which came in especially handy at a time like this. After a few inquiries, they learned of two possible spots where the kidnappers could be keeping Ellie. The truck was registered to an address just outside of Tahlequah, but the name on it was Henry Foster. It was possible that was Harrison's real name, but there was nothing too solid in that lead. Greg had also learned that Ted owned a cabin in a somewhat remote area not very far from a popular fishing spot. After Pax's discovery at the safe house, he knew this was the first place they needed to check.

They drove for several hours. The lower the sun set, the more anxious Pax became. Locating the poorly marked road leading them back to the cabin proved to be difficult, but after a couple of wrong turns, they found it. Pax motioned for Greg to slow down as their headlights streaked across what appeared to be another vehicle. They parked the little car behind some trees and cautiously approached two vehicles parked in front of a well-used trail. Pax recognized Ted's BMW right away. He wasn't sure about the other car, but he suspected that it had something to do with Harrison.

Pax and Greg carefully made their way toward the cabin. Lights were on inside, and smoke was rolling out of the chimney. As they got close, Greg pulled his revolver and pointed toward the back of the building. Pax nodded and made his way to the front door. He'd just reached the window next to the door when he heard a gunshot, and Ellie screamed.

Pax crouched down below the window and took a deep breath. He carefully stood up and peeked inside. Marcus was staggering back, holding his chest. Blood gushed from the wound beneath his fingers. Then, he fell backward and was still. Ellie sat near the fireplace, shock and terror evident on her face. Pax silently thanked God that Ellie hadn't been the one who was shot. Ted was holding the gun, looking at Marcus as if he were a rodent that needed to be disposed of. Pax had to get inside without Ted seeing him, but he wasn't quite sure how to do that yet.

Ellie sat with her hand over her mouth, looking at Marcus's body in horror. She shakily removed her hand and looked at Ted. "Why did you have to shoot him?" She had so many other questions, but she couldn't form the words at the moment.

Ted looked at Ellie and then walked back to the counter. He wiped his fingerprints off the gun and set it down. "I didn't shoot him, buttercup. Paxton did."

She shook her head, trying to deny the betrayal happening before her eyes. "You're as deluded as Marcus."

Ted laughed. "You wanna talk delusions, buttercup? Let's talk about your mother." He sat in the chair next to hers and gave her humorless smile. "She was fickle and indecisive. She was married to your dad, but she was sleeping with me. She never could decide which of us she wanted more. I guess it just depended on what mood she was in that day."

Ellie shook her head. A tear slid down her cheek. "No. You're lying."

Ted smiled at her. "I assure you I'm not. I begged her to leave Jacob, but she refused. She liked the money, which was something I didn't yet have." He stretched his legs out and crossed them, getting comfortable.

"Then, one day, she came to me, worried. She was pregnant. Under normal circumstances, that would have been no big deal, but this presented a large problem. Jacob couldn't have kids. They'd known for a couple of years. Once Jacob found out, he was livid. He threatened to kick her out. I was perfectly happy with the idea, but she wasn't."

Ted frowned as he looked into the fire. "Jacob loved Mary, but he couldn't stand the thought of raising my child as his own. He also hated the idea of someone knowing she'd been unfaithful, so they hid the truth. She spent the last trimester at a private health spa, waiting for the baby to arrive, and then they put him up for adoption. That would be that sorry excuse for a man you see lying on the floor over there. When she came back, she lied to me and said she'd lost the baby. As fate would have it, Marcus and his new family relocated to the area when he was five." He shook his head as he thought back. "I knew the moment I met Marcus that he was mine. He had characteristics that mimicked my own, and he had Mary's eyes. Once I verified that Marcus was adopted, I did some digging and learned the rest. But Mary wouldn't come clean about any of it." He sighed. "Anyway, once Marcus turned 18, I told him the truth, and the rest, as they say, is history."

Ted had just killed his biological son in cold blood, and he didn't even feel remorse. Ellie shuddered.

Ted saw the little movement she made and laughed. "I'm sure you're also wondering how you ended up in the Manchester family since Jacob had fertility issues."

She was too numb to find her voice, so she simply nodded.

Ted went to refill his coffee as he talked, "You were adopted, too. Mary mourned the loss of her newborn as if he really had died. It hurt her so much that Jacob decided they needed to find a replacement, so to speak. A few months later, they brought you home. I suppose they were gonna tell you someday, but after Mary died, I don't think Jacob had the guts to go through with it."

Ellie rubbed her temples. She had to fight the urge to scream at Ted. His words were turning her whole world upside down. She didn't want to hear anymore.

"I know you don't believe me, but it's true." He sat back down next to her and sighed. "Then, one night, I came to see your mom during a house party. I had repeatedly tried to get her to confess her deceit, but she never would. I'll admit to being very, very angry. She was a lying whore, and she needed to pay for all the misery she'd caused me. But then, you were there, weren't you, Ellie? You didn't see my face, but you were there. Of course, you were supposed to be in the playroom that night, but naughty little Ellie was always breaking the rules."

Ellie gasped and dropped her cup, the shards flying in several different directions as it hit the floor. *After all these years, how have I not known it was Ted?*

She leaned forward and slapped him hard. "You sick bastard!"

Ted rubbed his cheek and laughed. "I see you've gotten some of your spunk back. Good for you. You'll need it."

Ted stood up and kicked the shattered cup pieces out of his way. Then, he walked toward the counter where he'd placed the gun. He turned at the sound of a soft click coming from near the back door. Pax stood in the doorway, glaring at him, with a gun pointed in his direction.

"You're doing an awful lot of confessing there, Ted. You must be trying to make amends before I kill you, but I highly doubt there's any level of forgiveness for a scumbag like you."

Ted simply grinned at Pax. "No, I'm not seeking forgiveness. Just making sure she understands why she has to die, too." He held up his hands and took a step toward Pax. "You see, she broke up with Marcus and ruined his life, and then you came along. You fell in love and became obsessed with her. It's all in the kidnapping report I filed a few days ago."

Ted was especially proud of how his plan had taken shape. He'd hired Pax as a scapegoat, and he was doing exactly what Ted had expected of him.

"I came here and found that you and Marcus had fought over her. You shot him out of jealousy, but poor Ellie was accidentally shot, too, bleeding out right before your eyes. Shame. You just couldn't take the guilt of watching someone else you loved die, so you ended your own life as well. I tried to stop you, but I was just too late."

Ellie couldn't hold her tongue any longer. "Did you kill my father, too?"

Ted shook his head. "No, that was just a happy accident that worked in my favor. I did visit him that night, and I did slip some Valium into his whiskey bottle, but I have no idea how he ended up in that plane afterward. Knowing Jacob, he probably slept it off a bit and then went for his usual flight. Obviously, he wasn't yet sober enough to think clearly."

Pax's anger intensified. It was obvious he and Ellie had been a pawn in Ted's sick game this whole time. "Why kill Ellie, Ted? She was a victim of this mess as much as anyone."

Ted glanced at Ellie, never fully taking his eyes off of Pax. He frowned. "I'm sorry, buttercup, but I have to. You know the truth about your mother, and this plan doesn't work if you're alive to tell a different side of the story. I've spent twenty years waiting for you to remember something that would implicate me. I'm tired of living with that burden. Besides, with you gone, I end up with the business and the money. I win all the way around. I might have been able to do things differently had Jacob paid my blackmailing demands, but I think he was onto me."

Pax nodded. "He was. I have proof you were behind all the threatening letters—except the ones you had Marcus write, of course."

Ted's smile became distorted, and his features filled with menace. "You're lying, Paxton!"

It was Pax's turn to smile. "No, actually, I'm not, Ted. I have handwriting samples that prove it was you."

Ted continued to scowl. "Ha. I'll just have Harrison get rid of that."

Pax's smile grew wider, mostly because he knew it irritated Ted. "That'll be hard to do, seeing as my buddy Greg has Harrison tied up in the trunk of our car right now."

Ted's face was starting to turn red as his anger built.

"Besides," said Pax, "a copy of the results and all the other information I have has been sent to local authorities as well as to some of my friends in the FBI just in case your old buddies on the force decide to try to help you out."

Ted's anger surged, and he charged Pax, catching him slightly off guard.

Pax lost his grip on the gun, and it slid out of his reach. He wrapped his arms around Ted and pushed him backward. They hit the counter with a thud and then rolled to the floor. Ellie wanted to grab the gun and help, but she couldn't get to either man's gun without getting in their way. Ted managed to pin Pax down and started throwing punches, but his victory was short-lived. Pax rolled him and hit him repeatedly in the face until Ted was covered in blood.

Ellie ran to Pax and grabbed his arm just as he'd pulled back to hit Ted yet again. "Stop!"

Pax's rage had gotten the better of him, and he was on the verge of literally beating Ted to death. He held Ted's motionless body down with one arm while Ellie gripped the other.

"Pax, please look at me."

He looked into her face and saw fear.

"Pax, he's not worth it. Death is too easy for him. Let him rot in jail."

He knew she was right. They had more than enough evidence, including Ellie's statement, to put him away for life on charges of blackmail, kidnapping, and attempted murder—not to mention killing Marcus, which sealed his fate. Harrison might be willing to testify against Ted for a lesser sentence as well.

Pax gave Ted one last shove and stood up. Ellie stepped closer, and Pax pulled her into his arms.

She cried as he held her. "I was so worried about you! I was afraid you'd been hurt in the accident, or they'd killed you!"

Pax smoothed a hand over her hair and spoke softly, "I'm okay, beautiful. You're the one who was in danger. I'm sorry I couldn't stop this. Did they hurt you?"

She kept he face buried in his chest, but she shook her head.

Pax kissed the top of her head. "Damn, Ellie. I was afraid I might have been too late. I can't lose you. Ted had me pegged about one thing. I can't live without you."

She pulled back, and he rubbed a thumb over her tear-streaked cheek.

She gently kissed him and then looked into his eyes. "I love you, Pax. I was afraid to admit it, but I do. I think I always have."

Pax could hardly believe his ears. *She loves me?* He'd wanted to hear those words for weeks, but he'd never fully expected them. He knew she cared, but he wasn't sure she would allow herself to love again. "You have no idea how badly I've wanted to hear you say that."

She smiled at him again and moved in to give him another kiss when she caught movement out of the corner of her eye. She didn't have time to think. She just reacted. The gun Ted had used on Marcus was within reach, so she grabbed it.

Ted was behind Pax, a kitchen knife in hand, and he was ready to strike. She pointed the gun at Ted and fired. Pax instantly pulled her into the protection of his arms out of instinct, not realizing she was the one who'd fired the shot.

Ted dropped the knife, a look of shock on his face. "Ellie?" he whispered as he fell.

Ellie looked down at the body of the man she'd always thought of as an uncle and realized she felt nothing but relief.

19

Pax and Ellie walked through the door of her apartment, exhaustion evident on both of their faces. She walked into the kitchen, grabbed a new bottle of wine, and sat on the sofa.

Pax sat next to her and smiled. "No glass?"

She grinned at him. "After trying to explain all of that to the police? This is a straight-from-the-bottle kind of night."

He laughed and put an arm around her, pulling her to him. Ellie placed her head on his shoulder and closed her eyes, enjoying the safety of his arms. Her mind had been racing over the events of her past.

None of it was her fault. Even Marcus had partially been a setup. She'd met him after coming home from college. They had become friends, and before long, they had started dating. After they'd broken up, she'd felt he'd only dated her because he had been hoping to end up with company someday, but it was Ted he had really been trying to please.

To give Marcus credit, she believed he had genuinely developed feelings for her—obsessive, weird stalker feelings, but feelings nonetheless. When it was all said and done, he'd refused to follow Ted's orders to kill her, which had ended in his death instead.

A tiny part of her felt sad for Marcus. Maybe he could have eventually moved on and found someone to make him happy.

She sighed out loud.

Pax heard her sigh and used his index finger to lift her chin. His eyes were full of worry. "Are you really okay, Ellie?"

She nodded sadly. "I'm fine. I just need to adjust to the revelation that my whole life has been a lie—even my childhood."

Pax gently kissed her. "There might have been people in your life with dishonest motives, but that doesn't make anything about your life a lie. Your parents still loved you. You still dealt with tragedy, grief, and sorrow. You still have wonderful, happy memories. You just didn't have all the information they did. In this case, that might not be a bad thing."

She tried to view her life from that angle. It was difficult, but maybe someday, that would be her truth. It would take time, but she imagined that as long as Pax was there, she could move on. She kissed him again, dropping the unopened bottle of wine on the floor.

Pax smiled as she climbed onto his lap. "What about the wine?"

She shook her head. "I don't need wine. I just need you."

He pulled her head to his and kissed her with all the passion and love he knew how to show. Then, he leaned her back on the cushions and placed himself on top of her, her legs straddling his hips. She laughed as he kissed his way down her neck.

"Have I ever told you how much I love your laugh?"

She laughed again. "No, I don't think you have."

Pax rose up and looked at her. "I love your laugh. I love your smile. I love the way you twirl your hair when you're thinking." He gently stroked a long curl through his fingers and let it fall. "I love everything about you, Ellie, absolutely everything. You're damn near perfect."

She shook her head in denial, but she was glad he saw past her faults. "I love you, too, Pax. You're amazing, brave, and unselfish. I hope to be more like you someday."

He stared at her lips. "I'm not feeling very unselfish right now."

She was confused. "You don't? Why?"

He looked back up to her eyes and then sat up. His face was so serious that it worried her.

"Pax?"

"This isn't how I planned to do this, Ellie. I was going to wait, but I can't."

He was being vague, and it was about to drive her crazy. "What the hell are you talking about?"

Pax stood up and then took her hand. She followed him into the bedroom, and he stopped just inside the doorway. He led Ellie around to stand in front of him, and then he backed her against the door. She was caught off guard, but her mind flashed back to that night when he'd first kissed her.

He pressed his whole body against her and said, "I'm feeling very selfish. I don't want to share you—ever." He kissed her with urgency that spoke of his need for her. "I've replayed this moment in my mind often. I kept kicking myself for doing it wrong. I wanted to tell you so many things, but none of it came out right. Consider this a do-over."

Ellie smiled at him. "You don't need a do-over, Pax."

He kissed her ear and then her neck. His hands worked their way underneath her shirt and then around to her lower back to press her closer. "I do, Ellie. I need to tell you what I should have told you then."

She tried to comprehend his meaning while attempting not to sigh over the way he was caressing her skin.

He pushed his forehead to hers. "Ellie, I'm in love with you. The moment you doused me with hot coffee, I think I knew you were the love of my life."

Ellie gasped. "It *was* hot! You told me it wasn't!"

He put his finger to her lips. "Hush. That's not the important part."

She nodded and let him continue.

"After the incident at the flea market, I realized that the tables had turned. In the beginning, you needed me and didn't even know it. Then, you were almost taken, and I realized that, in truth, I needed you. And I swear on my dying breath that if we had solved all this mess way back then, I would have made up excuses to be around you. In reality, you saved me. I was slowly dying inside until I met you. I'd given up on being happy, but you make me happy. I hope I make you happy, too."

She nodded, a tear of joy sliding down her face. Ellie never believed she could be this happy.

He kissed her where the tear fallen, and then he looked into her eyes. "Elizabeth Manchester, I know we've been through a lot, and not all of it has been good. But I'd love to spend the rest of my life making it up to you, if you'll let me."

Her eyes grew wide.

Pax's courage faltered a bit, but he continued on, "Marry me, Ellie. You're a beautiful rare flower, and I don't deserve you. I'm a boring simple vase. But if my only job is to spend the rest of my life holding you, then I will die a very happy man."

Ellie pulled him close and whispered, "Yes, Pax, absolutely yes. But you have to promise me one thing."

Pax nodded and said, "Anything."

She gave him a seductive smile. "We have to end every argument with you pressing me against this door."

Pax laughed. "I'll plan on doing lots of arguing then."

Ellie laughed, too.

Then, they shared a kiss that would be the beginning of many more to come.

The End

ACKNOWLEDGMENTS

I can honestly say that I never truly believed I would someday have the privilege of writing this page. Getting here took an astounding amount of hard work and time, and I would be remiss not to say a huge thank you to those who helped make it possible.

My husband, John, has always been my biggest supporter. Without him, I would not have had the courage to attempt this dream. My two children have also cheered me on throughout the process, and they even enjoyed giving me ideas and advice. They endured late meals and my sometimes frazzled nerves. All three of you have been my rock, and I love you more than life itself. Thank you for being as excited about this as I am and for pushing me to succeed.

My parents and siblings have always been supportive of my dreams, whatever they might be. Thank you all for fostering my creativity and cheering me on. A special thanks to my sister, Lana, who has talked me off of the ledge a time or two. I love you all!

Many thanks to my beta readers—Lana, Paula, Kari, Polly, Tania, Danielle, Tammy, Becky, and Ailsa. You ladies were instrumental in helping me to stay on topic and true to my characters. Thank you for your honesty and time.

Thank you to Paula Love for her knowledge and enthusiasm during the editing process. You were invaluable to this project.

Many thanks to Jovana Shirley for her excellent editing and design skills, for squeezing me into her schedule, and for being patient with me as I learned about this entire crazy process. You're the best!

Thanks to Sarah Hanson for the amazing cover work. Your talent knows no bounds, and I'm honored to have worked with you.

I also owe a sincere thanks to my childhood friend Jamie McGuire. She has been encouraging and patient with me as I occasionally bombarded her with questions. I owe you a drink and a hug, dear lady!

A huge thanks to you, my readers, who make all this possible. I will be forever grateful that you joined me on this journey. I hope you enjoyed reading this book as much as I enjoyed writing it. I'll have many more stories to come, but Pax and Ellie will always hold a special place in my heart. Thanks for taking a chance on us. Pax and Ellie appreciate it almost as much as I do.

ABOUT THE AUTHOR

Amy Hale is an Oklahoma native now living in Illinois. Her husband and two children are the center of her universe—although her cat believes otherwise. She's been writing stories and poems since childhood, providing an outlet for her active imagination. She loves music, reading, writing, and photography. Amy believes that happiness comes from surrounding yourself with people you love, helping others, and being content with your current place in the world.

You can find Amy in the following places:
Website: www.authoramyhale.com
Facebook: www.facebook.com/authoramyhale
Twitter: @AuthorAmyHale

Made in the USA
Charleston, SC
31 January 2015